MURDER MOST TERRIBLE!

by

CHARLES NUETZEL

WRITING AS "FRED MACDONALD"

The Borgo Press
An Imprint of Wildside Press

MMVII

SECOND EDITION

Contents

Introduction

Story ideas come from strange places and circumstances. Not always full blown; and sometimes only with a vague concept, a setting, a seed. It can come from nothing but a visual impression, a moment in time that would normally have passed as nothing more than a nice, pleasant morning.

I remember the beach, ocean reaching out to the horizon, the sun baking bright and hot over the town of Santa Monica, California. And for some reason I thought about those islands out there, just peaking up from the blue ocean. For some reason it struck me as a neat setting for a book. Now, there must a story there somewhere! But beyond that feeling, there was nothing; no germ of an idea. But certainly this was a beginning.

So, like any dutiful writer, desperate for an idea for a story, the next time I sat down at my monster typewriter I fed it with paper and typed: CHAPTER ONE, went down a few spaces and wrote:

"Very few people have heard of the small island off the California coast."

And I was off and running. Well, sorta. It took a little more than the cute little "bikini-clad girl in her early twenties" to spark more than a mild interest in what kind of cutes she might offer up to my main character.

Well, truth is, I came up with a *Murder Most Terrible* involving a young woman and her brother....

A man I named Bill Johnson.

Well that was a better start. Now I had two characters. What next? Let's see. Where's he going in this small boat with this cute bikini-clad girl, and why are they going there? Questions and questions, but no answers. Well, this young lady is sexy—to boot. And he's not about to boot her into the ocean! Rather pull her into his arms, protectively, natch! Of course! Sure. If you believe that you'll believe anything!

Hmmm...well, we have a sexy little issue here. So maybe the island they are going to is a place of Eros...well, we'll just call it Eros Island.

My, how ideas fly in an author's face like the wind blows across the ocean waves. Well, okay, not his, but ol' Bill Johnson's, who happens to have a sister...

Gosh, I don't want to get ahead of the game and give the story up before it has even been read!

But we can tease you with the fact that he discovered that the island is involved in a cult devoted to Pagan Rites. Why, as our hero soon discovers, some people actually lived there year around, while others just came on weekends for wild parties, no holds barred.

Actually, ideas were flying wildly in my head, and I was imagining all sorts of wonderful and exciting things that had little to do with *Murder Most Terrible*! So it was time to complicated matters.

There is far more to things going on here than just a seedy swinging club of wild people on a weekend orgy.

Suddenly things began to get interesting, as the real secret of this cult was exposed followed by another *Murder Most Terrible!*

—CHARLES NUETZEL
Thousand Oaks, California
July 2006

Chapter One

Very few people have heard of the small island off the California coast, some twenty miles beyond U.S. Government authority, where the Castle of Eros was constructed to house a cult devoted to the practice of total sexual freedom. Members of the Cult of Eros were carefully picked and kept its secrets. To the rest of the world it simply didn't exist.

I approached the island called Eros by motor, captained by a young bikini-clad girl in her early twenties named Michael Corning, Mic or Mike to all her friends.

She had been a friend of my sister's, but she didn't know my true identity at the time. I was going by the name of William Johnson, which was merely a reversal of my real name: John Williamson.

I figured it would be possible to "pick her brains" while getting to the island. But I hadn't taken into account the very nature of the Pagan Cult she belonged to. I didn't, at that point, fully understand what I was getting into. Soon I'd know; sooner than I had expected.

This young woman was one hell of a prime sampling of what would soon follow. More than I could have imagined.

Mic was a small, bouncy, freckle-faced college girl who looked no more than sixteen. She wore a white bikini, hardly more than two strips of cloth that displayed her body almost to the point of nudity. Long red hair flowed freely in the breeze as the boat raced across the coastal waters of the blue Pacific.

The realization that before the weekend was over I would probably be making love to this delightful young woman created an automatic desire to do so, instantly. A man couldn't look at Mic, half naked as she was, without that kind of reaction.

We weren't more than a mile from land when Mic put the boat on full automatic and turned to me.

"Well, Billy, I must say you'll make an exciting addition to our membership." Her eyes flashed meaningfully along my body.

I found it totally impossible to ignore her thrusting breasts, whose nipples were just barely hidden behind the white cloth. It was a sight meant invite stares. She had a lovely narrow waist, a rounded stomach and flaring hips. Her legs were what one might call softly muscular, exciting.

"You're not bad yourself, Mic," I countered huskily, trying hard to appear casual about it.

"You like me?" Mic inquired, delighted, taking a sensual pose that thrust out her breasts and hips all at once. The boat wasn't too large, but big enough so that it was easy to consider the idea of a rather interesting party for two.

"Who wouldn't?" I offered, honestly.

"You know, Bill," she announced, starting to reach around to the back of her bikini top, "It's amazing how our little group keeps getting new members. You say that you knew a friend of Judy's?"

"In the Army," I told her, my voice becoming husky as I realized what she was about to do.

The bikini top slipped off large bouncy breasts, whose nipples were cherry pink. My throat went suddenly dry.

Judy, my sister, had written about the club she'd joined. I was stunned out of my wits by her last letters, which told exactly what kind of action it offered; it was one thing for a man to play loose sexual games, but a jolt to learn his kid sister was enjoying a swinging life-style on a pleasure island devoted to free wheeling sex.

Now, standing before me, breasts boldly naked to my gaze, was Judy's room-mate, the girl who had originally introduced her to the club.

"Judy was one of the best, an all around girl. She went in for all the kicks. I'll tell you one thing, there was no one more popular It was terrible when she was...killed. Nobody knows for sure who did it."

I fought down the emotional welling pain that cut at me. The first shock of hearing of Judy's death, only a couple of weeks before my discharge from the Army, was still like an open wound. I focus all my attention to Mic's naked breasts, as a pleasing distraction.

"You think they're nice?" Mic inquired, suddenly.

For a moment I didn't have the least idea what she was talking about. Then, when she laughed and placed hands under her breasts, I got the idea.

"About as nice as they come," I admired, moistening my dry lips. The blood was throbbing at my temples at the mere sight of those large mounds of flesh and their taut nipples.

Mic's green eyes took on a pleased, haunting glow. There was something of the pixie look about her. She had an up-swept freckled nose. Even her breasts had freckles on them.

"How much do you know about our club?" Mic inquired, sitting down beside me at the end of the boat.

"Well, from what I've learned about the Cult of Eros, it lives up to its name."

"In spades!" Her laugh was light, girlish. "What else?"

"Well, membership is, if I'm not wrong, a thousand dollars a year for outsiders, fifty a night or day, for casuals—and two hundred a month for the girls who live at the castle, five hundred for the men. Is that about right?"

Mic nodded. "You are well informed. You know about the rites?"

"Not too much," I lied.

"Well, you'll find out tonight. Val—she's the King's daughter—will do her dance of passion and no doubt take you on first. That is usually the routine. She's a real swinger. There isn't anything she won't do. I think you'll like her."

This boldly un-jealous statement jarred me. I tried hard to keep from eyeing Mic's luscious fleshy breasts, but they were too close to ignore. It would be so easy to just reach out and cover one with the palm of my hand.

She turned, looked up at me. "You'll learn all about Val, tonight. She likes it with both girls and

12

boys. Doesn't really care which. She's been after me for some time—but I haven't decided to go that route as yet. The other day, do you know, she caught me in the living room—we were alone, and I was dressed something like this—and Val comes over and says, *Dear, you have the best breasts in the group. Let me touch them.* Just like that she says it. But that's Val for you. One gets used to it, so I teased her a little. I cupped my breasts like this," and her hands pressed them upwards so that the nipples were extended as if tempting a kiss. "She got so excited that before I could do anything she was kissing them. Darned if it didn't feel good! I'll admit that. But then…they are erotically sensitive, of course. And in the dark, I suppose, one wouldn't know the dif."

Mic's eyes looked at me. "Damned if it doesn't excite me thinking about it. I don't want to go lez the route—but lips are lips. Don't you think that's so? If somebody knows how to kiss them, it probably doesn't make much difference, do you think?"

By now my own restraint was in a shambles. She was still holding her breasts in the same manner, the nipples pressed outwards, their points like little needles. Her eyes were eagerly inviting, questioning.

She looked up at the sky for a moment, then back to my body. "Aren't you a little hot, under all that clothing?"

In more ways than one, I realized.

"Why don't you undress? I'm not bashful, and you'd better learn to be a little more relaxed. You look like you're about to explode." She dropped her hands away from those lovely breasts. "I guess that does bother a man, doesn't it?"

"It was meant to, wasn't it, Mic?" I countered, starting to pull off my blue sweater, all the time looking into her eyes.

She laughed, brightly. "I guess so!"

I pulled off my T-shirt and Mic's eyes grew large. "You're sure well-built, Bill—built to the hilt—I would imagine." Her eyes fairly burned across my body.

"How much longer to the island?" I inquired starting to sit down next to her.

"Take off your pants, Bill—after all, you won't be any more naked than I am."

Her suggestion was startling, and for a moment I could hardly move because of the sudden surge of desire that flushed across me. There was no doubt that she wanted me to make love to her, right there on the boat.

"We have plenty of time," Mic announced. "And to be honest...well, you know what kind of club we have, and there's no reason to let Val have all the firsties, is there? But, for God's sake, don't let out what's happened. Val would be furious."

Her boldness had become blunt.

"I know you want to kiss them," she said, touching the tips of each of her breasts. "Everybody does! I want you to."

I tried to tell myself that, fantastic as it might seem, Mic might have been the one who killed my sister. It could have been anybody on the island; all were suspect. And that's what was going there to discover: my sister's murderer.

Stepping out of my slacks, I moved down next to Mic, who now cupped her breasts in open offer-

14

ing, pressing out the nipples for my lips to kiss.

It seemed quite natural, though highly wanton, for her to make this offer, I realized as my lips touched one of her breasts. We had met only an hour before—but considering the type of place Eros was, why shouldn't she start such games right off?

The taste of her flesh was salty from the ocean spray and when she suddenly released her hold on the breasts and grabbed my head in her hands, moving me back and forth from one nipple to the other, a blast of desire flushed away all thoughts about her being one of many murder suspects. There was little doubt in my mind that I would be in such situations with each woman on the island. And after several years in the Army, most of it spent at places where there were few women, the idea was less than undesirable.

"Do it some more," Mic murmured, directing my head across her breasts again. "I'll just slip out of these little old things while you continue."

I hesitated, started to move my hands to her hips, where the bikini bottom was located. She slapped my hands away.

"Naughty boy! For shame! What kind of girl do you think I am?" she teased in a very serious voice. Then laughingly added: "Let me get them off. I'm better at it. And I want your kisses to keep me excited." She giggled and wriggled while my lips feasted on her plump, young breasts. Then I felt her fingers work under the elastic of my underpants.

After that it was only a short time before she embraced me with willing arms.

"Now, Bill, let me know you completely. I'm really ready for all of you...so make it good, big muscles." She clutched gently at me, her hips moved up to meet mine, and with amazing skill directed our forms together in the first gentle union. Her firm calves locked to mine in one fluid motion that only long practice could have perfected.

"Oh, Bill, this is going to be good. Just lie still, let the boat...the boat will do it all." She kissed my neck, then her lips found mine and a small pointed tongue leaped in deep as she strained closer, her supple breasts cushioning against the muscles of my chest.

"You feel delicious," she murmured a moment later. "Just delicious."

Then movement that was not caused by the rocking of the boat started to surge through her body and I could feel the tension of passion taking control of her muscles. Sobs of delight started to break past her trembling, red lips.

"God of Lust, good, good, good." Her voice accented every movement her body made. Then as the pleasure rocketed skyward to the exploding point, she went rigid and trembled convulsively. After that I knew such great pleasure that it left me exhausted beyond movement.

Shortly afterwards, Mic urged me away from her. "You'd better get dressed, we're getting close to the island. And promise to say nothing about this to the others."

Suddenly I realized that my plans on questioning Mic about Judy had turned into a total failure. This was why I had contacted Mic. I had to find out who was responsible for my kid sister's death and then see that justice was dealt out.

As I stood, Mic grabbed her bikini and started

16

slipping into the panties.

I gathered up my clothing and looked out across the horizon. Straight ahead, less than a mile away, was the small point of an island, not much more than a large double rock formation, which I later learned had a tiny beach. Between the bold, rounded pillars of rock, I could see a Gothic-type tower—the castle of Eros.

"We have a real party planned for you tonight," she announced in an excited voice. "They will always do it up good for a new member. But you'll have to see the King first."

Chapter Two

Andrew King was dressed in fine, silken robes that fell colorfully about his huge frame. The King, Andy King, or Father, as he was alternately called, was a very large man in his fifties, with long white hair, a full, white beard and thin, wine-colored lips. His beady, fanatic eyes, which looked bluish gray, glared out of an angular face with a large, strong nose. Bushy eye-brows knitted together as he gazed at me. This was the Master of Eros.

I had been taken directly to the castle, which was a large, double towered building of stone with arched doorways. The doors themselves were made of thick, hand-carved hardwood. The room in which the Master was granting this first interview was large. One wall was a solid bookcase from floor to ceiling. From the few titles I'd been able to make out, it was filled with highly erotic literature. On the other wall hung beautiful paintings, Greek, Chinese and European art, all erotic in theme. A huge desk stood in the center of the room, and from the ceiling overhead hung a brightly lit chandelier of glittering glass.

Mic had brought me to the room through an empty house of large rooms and high-ceilinged hallways, all wood paneled, decorated by modem art and lovely statues of nudes, both men and women, usually in sexual embraces.

"Welcome, my son," Andrew King's resonant voice boomed at me through the room, almost bouncing back on itself. "We are honored that you have heard of our humble society and wish to join us in the search for ultimate ecstasy, that state in which all humans were born to seek out and enjoy." He embraced me with a large, almost smothering hug, the purplish red robes totally covering my head. Then he stepped away.

"Be comfortable. This can be as your home. Seat yourself, my son." He made a grand movement with his right arm, indicating a large leather chair. "It folds back, press the button on its side and it will vibrate deliciously."

With giant steps, as if he were walking on eggs and wished not to break any more than necessary, King moved around the huge desk and sat on his own chair. His large hands folded together on the neat, almost empty desk top.

"Well, now, son, tell me how you learned about our place." His eyes probed mine as if attempting to read my thoughts.

"A friend, of Judy Williamson's told me about it. I was in the service with him, and he mentioned this...organization. We spent many nights talking about your...organization—and I must admit the very idea made life a little bit better in that long hitch in South Vietnam. Now, in all honesty, I look forward to enjoying the pleasures of membership."

"All in due time, my son." King grew thoughtful for a moment. "It was terrible what happened to dear little Judy. She was one of the most popular members of our society. She enjoyed all the fruits we offered. There are seldom such women who so willingly feast upon the total pleasures of a sensual life. A bitter shame, her loss."

"What happened to her?" I inquired, attempting to make it sound casual.

"She was murdered—so it would seem from the bare facts. She was found on the beach one morning, her head crushed in. She'd apparently been with a man not long before being killed. There wasn't a stitch of clothing on the lovely girl. But that's hardly unusual here," he added.

"You said murdered? Did they discover who did it?"

"No...there is no authority other than ourselves here, and we did conduct an investigation— but found no evidence to point to anybody. It could have been anybody here. What *can* I do? Hang every member? It is best we forget the whole matter. My guess is that somebody accidentally killed her."

"Then why call it murder?"

"The Bible says that death by one's own hand to another is murder most terrible."

His quote was hardly accurate.

"Doesn't it bother you?" I asked, "knowing that somebody here committed murder?"

"Murder is a strong word; perhaps I was wrong in using it. As I said, her head was crushed in, but that might have happened accidentally. But enough of this. Things have been running smoothly since then. It was the first and last such incident. We have a new ruling: Any time great emotions attack a person, they are to come here and have a chat with me, or go to some other member of the group, who will listen and soothe the emotional tension through the art of love. If jealousies develop, if arguments start to take place, go then to another!" He smiled broadly. "But this is hardly the time to be speaking such morbid words. Tell me what you know of our society."

I took a deep breath, then stated: "I have been told that you search out the truth through total use of the senses—the complete oneness of man. Sensual pleasures are considered the reaching out toward God. The closer one comes to ultimate pleasure with another, giving, sharing, of one's total being, the submitting of self to the pleasures of another's body, the nearer one comes to the final perfection that God created us to become."

His eyebrows rose high. "You quote our book with great insight. Where did you come across that?"

I told him from Judy's friend, though it had actually been from a letter she had written to me while I was in the service.

He nodded. "You speak good words. You are well grounded in our total reason for being. As you know there is a fee for membership. But there are several kinds of fees, and I must ask you what kind of union you seek with us."

My answer was well practiced, for I knew exactly what was required and what would be needed to do a complete investigation concerning my sister's death. I'd had plenty of time to prepare.

"I would like to live here and enjoy the complete union which your society offers, for it is my understanding that only in that way is it possible to approach total oneness with the Spirit of all Man."

He nodded. "Now, let me ask you some pointed questions, and I expect honest answers."

"Do you mind if I smoke?"

"Do as you wish, my son," he told me, "here we are all adults seeking the perfection of life, and all that gives pleasure is ours for the asking."

He leaned back in the chair, looked up at the ceiling, his hands clasped together as if in prayer.

"Tell me, my son, what experiences have you had so far in your life, in the pleasures of the body?"

"I don't quite understand the question," I countered carefully.

"Well, I'll ask questions that come to the point, then. Have you ever experienced oneness with another man—or boy?"

An inner shudder crept through me. "I guess everybody has tried that as a young child—well, as a very young man."

"Did you find it pleasurable?"

"At the time I guess I did...though now I must admit to a preference for the female sex."

The older man chuckled. "There are those among us who would rather enjoy a man than a woman—there are some who seek pleasure with both. Many of the girls go in for anything, for once they have learned that the sensations of the body do not depend upon the sex of the person giving that pleasure, but more to the feelings exchanged...well, you'll discover. For now, that's enough of an explanation."

I thought about one of the letters Judy had sent me and quoted it almost totally. "It seems to me that sexual practices between members of the same sex are like...well, say, having a juicy hamburger—better than dog food—which might be compared to finding pleasure with oneself—but that heterosexual experience is like a good steak."

"That is substantially my own belief. I never did go in for boys, myself. But I do not look down upon those who wish hamburgers rather than expensive steaks. I prefer fine wines, imported and expensive, rather than the cheap beer. I would rather have a banquet of delicious roasts, fowl, stuffed pig, with wine sauces smothering the vegetables, than simple hamburger, but I do not look down upon those whose tastes are more plebian than mine. Union, no matter how one seeks it and finds it, is better than loneness. To be together with another soul, no matter who or what, is far better than being alone. To be shared is better than to selfishly deny the total being and love one can give others."

He patted the desk before him. "Well, my son. Business. It takes money to keep our society moving. As a special introductory tryout period, it'll be four hundred a month, the first two months in advance will give you complete freedom within our castle of Eros. You will drink of the wines and stronger liquids of the gods and you will feast upon the foods, be they for the stomach or for the emotions and body. You have the fee with you?"

I nodded and took out my wallet. It was all the money I had in the world, but figured that before a month had passed I would have discovered my, sister's murderer.

After receiving my cash fee, Andrew King slipped it into a drawer, then smiled benevolently.

"My son, remember, that the castle is your home. Do here as you wish. On weekends we have many guests who come to enjoy a couple of days of total giving to one another, and you will learn the joys of totally giving yourself. But you are never forced to share with one who is undesirable to you. In time, the complete awareness of selfless giving will come upon you and an amazing change will take place in your viewpoint about sharing. There is none to whom I would not give myself totally, for in the sharing is the receiving of a blessing from Heaven itself."

I didn't bother to mention the fact that I had no plans on staying put that long. I'm basically an old fashioned type who finds a woman delightful, but men slightly on the disagreeable side when one thinks of them as sexual partners.

"Well, son, I'll have one of our members show you around the house." He stood and led me out of the office study, and down the long, wood-paneled hall. Directing me into a huge living room, with a great stone fire-place, and thick carpets whose walls were decorated by beautifully designed modern murals, he added: "This is the meeting room for after-dinner cocktails—where casuals will be greeted by the household membership."

There were two women sitting on large sofas that stretched out across the middle of the room. One of them was small, with short black hair. As she turned to look at us, King said: "This is Sue Kong, she is second generation Chinese—and this is Rita Roselanda," he announced with a wave of his hand toward the other woman.

Rita was Latin, a little on the plump side, with

huge breasts and wide hips. Her broad mouth was large and invitingly sensual. Her bright eyes surveyed my body with open admiration. She appeared to be in her early thirties.

She was dressed in a long flowery peasant skirt and flaring white blouse that fluffed about her large bosom. It was an interesting sight.

Sue Kong was wearing a tight-fitting sweater against which her nipples were pressing in a very obvious manner. Shorts left bare two lovely, graceful legs.

"Rita," King's voice boomed, "Bill Johnson is a new member of our household and I thought you would enjoy the pleasure of showing him around. Let him pick an unoccupied room upstairs." He turned to me one last time and said: "Take of anything you wish at any time, my son. Anything offered is yours to bless!"

Then he motioned Sue Kong. "Come, child, I would show you that book you were interested in the other day. We will enjoy the afternoon exploring its possibilities."

Sue Kong slipped from the green sofa and glided to King's side. The contrast between the two was shocking. Sue was so tiny, King looked like some giant brute beast by comparison. I could hardly picture the two of them in physical union.

Rita stood and her breasts bounced wildly, dancing free under the blouse. Her generous lips opened wide and a pointed tongue moistened them. "Well, hello, Billy. I think you are going to enjoy our little place—and I'm going to do everything possible to make your tour interesting."

She took one of my arms and placed it under

hers, flush against the large outer swell of her breast. She was a lovely creature, hefty to say the least, but narrow-waisted and with tapering ankles. It was exciting to think of being intimate with this Latin dish. She appeared to be before dinner goodies, main course, and dessert all wrapped up in one delightful package.

"Come, I'll show you everything. Since we are going to live here together, I think we should become fast friends as soon as possible." Her large eyes looked up at mine, sparkling with promise.

"I'd like that," I admitted, feeling desire flood through my veins, "I think I'd like that a lot."

MURDER MOST TERRIBLE! BY CHARLES NUETZEL

Chapter Three

The Castle of Eros was a rambling place of many large rooms. The ground floor was devoted to meeting room, libraries—much like the one in King's study—art rooms, a music room, rooms with huge sofas and backless lounges. The most interesting of rooms of all was the main lounge, decorated in Roman style with a dais in the center upon which stood a large circular, padded couch, actually a round bed for four. Ionic pillars were along each wall and at each corner. Huge, beautifully painted murals were colorfully designed upon the walls, depicting men and women in Roman togas in the midst of a wild orgy.

"This," Rita announced, sitting on the round couch, "is where we will have our rites tonight. The Dance of Passion will start the ceremonies that won't end until late Sunday night. Everybody will meet in here and end up in the rooms upstairs in couples or triples, depending on what kind of situations develop."

She stretched out on her back, looking at the high ceiling. Her breasts rose and fell rapidly, a very inviting sight that tempted one to see them in total nudity.

"You know," she laughed, looking at me, "It can be a lot of fun. I mean, when there are more than just...well, I'm a big girl and sometimes I'm excited by the idea of more than one guy. That happened last weekend. Two big male animals feasted fully upon the delights I offered them." She winked. "It is good to share oneself fully, don't you think?"

"Isn't that what we're devoted to, here?" I agreed, watching her body. It was exciting to think about making the scene with Rita; a possibility I was beginning to realize might take place any moment, considering the hot expression in her large dark eyes.

"I have big passions, Billy. Big enough for more than one man. I like all the passions of Eros. Tell me, have you ever seen a woman with my body? I mean, I do have a large body, big enough to take on all lovers, embrace them completely all at once. I'm a big girl, don't you think?" She sat up, her breasts bouncing through an erotic dance. She lifted her hair high up on her head, stretching the large breasts upwards. It was a sight to drive any man's lusts to the point of wildness. She was openly flirting in a raw, sensual way with her whole body. And making no effort to be coy in any way. She was being brazen and totally open.

"You're certainly lovely, Rita," I admitted, though my preference in women was usually a slightly less voluptuously plump body than hers. Nonetheless, erotic desire was blasting through my nerves at that moment. We were totally alone in a large room that was fairly screaming sex.

There was another side of racing thoughts driving through my mind; confused, and also wildly delighted. I hadn't, really, thought about my own reaction to this Island of Erotica, merely recognized what would be required; a willingness to enjoy all its offering pleasures. Not until being there, like with Rita at that very moment, did I fully get the impact of what would be in expected of me. Any healthy young male would find the obvious situation more than seductive. And even many, if not most women. And that had included my sister. And she had been considered one of the most popular treats being offered up.

That last created very mixed feelings inside my gut. I pushed that away. And with little effort refocused my attention on the rather sultry charms of this hot Latin dish.

"Come on down here with me, sit a while." Her voice was sultry. Her right hand patted the huge circular bed. As I sat down, she loosened the blouse, pulling it from the skirt.

Taking my hand, she boldly slipped it under the blouse, pressing the fingers against a huge mound of yielding flesh, I felt a large nipple.

"I like to be touched that way." She smiled broadly. "You can touch and explore, I don't mind."

I controlled the impulse to rip the blouse away from her body. My fingers were fondling and exploring the amazingly generous breasts.

"Hey, you do that good!" she said as she moved closer, pulling my head to that large mouth. "I'm going to like you."

Her lips parted under mine, large, soft cushions of warm moist flesh. The point of her tongue teased mine, invited me to explore the depths of her mouth. It was a heady, passionate kiss, sending blood racing like mad through my body.

"Come," she urged a moment later, leaping to her feet, "Let me show you the rest of the house."

I let this plump bundle of sex appeal lead me from the room. We moved up a large spiral staircase to the second floor.

"Here are the bedrooms," she announced, squeezing my fingers.

The sound of giggling came from a room with the door partly open. Rita led the way to the door and looked in, totally unashamed.

On the bed two totally naked female forms were locked in a highly erotic embrace. The bodies trembled and soft moans of pleasure murmured through the air.

"Hello," Rita greeted the other girls with a giggle.

The two women paused for a moment, then after looking our way returned their attention to caressing and kissing one another.

Rita shrugged, then urged me from the door. The sight had unsettled me more because she had let them know we were watching and that they didn't seem to care in the least.

Like a zombie I allowed Rita to take me along the hall. Her words gushed out, but I heard nothing she said. Finally we came to a stop in front of a door.

"Would you like to see my room?" she invited. Without waiting for my answer, Rita opened the door, then fairly shoved me in, closing the door behind her.

"This," she announced with pride, "is where I sleep and where I join in the total oneness of spirit.

Try the bed, see how comfortable it is."

The bed had hand-carved backrests and night-stands. A hand-carved chest was on the opposite side of the room. A huge picture of a bull fighter faced the door.

Rita fairly shoved me to the large double bed. Sitting down, as instructed, I looked up at the woman.

In one fluid movement she pulled off her blouse. The sight of her naked breasts sent hot waves to flush through me. She had huge breasts, firm and full, the nipples spread out, large chestnut ovals over the balloon-like supple flesh.

"I was bored before you came in," she announced, standing in front of me. "One look at you and I said to myself, 'things are getting better all the time. I see no reason to let Val be the first one with you.' Why shouldn't we share total togetherness?"

Her big breasts were only inches from my face, bobbing up and down with every word she spoke.

Suddenly she embraced my head in soft, plump arms, smothering my face in that mass of yielding flesh. For a moment I felt panic. It was possible to be actually smother to death against her.

"Come," she said, releasing my head, "I'll slip out of these things and we'll do it right." She was now panting heavily, her breasts dancing up and down, fairly vibrating.

All thoughts were totally burned away with the hot offer of this woman's body. All I could think of was relieving the pain that was hurting like hell.

She slipped out of her skirt. The garter-belt that held up sheer nylon stockings was bright red, pulled tight across her wide hips and rounded belly.

"Do you want to?" she offered, indicating her stockings and garter belt.

I automatically reached out, touched the nylons, and then reached up to the soft naked flesh of her thigh.

"I think..." my voice managed huskily, "You'd better. I'll get undressed."

Actually shaking, I started following Rita's example, until both of us were ready to share total oneness.

She appraised me with her bright eyes, "You are going to be good, I bet."

Then she reached out and her hand touched my shoulder, feeling the hard muscle. Her other hand pressed me back on the bed. "Let me show you some tricks," she offered, moving close so that our hips were touching. "That is going to make you feel very good."

Abruptly she was moving down toward me and it was almost alarming. It wasn't so much she was heavy, but merely so largely proportioned. Her breasts dangled over my face, inviting kisses that were impossible to hold back.

Her tongue licked out over those generous lips, licking back and forth with voluptuous pleasure as I feasted upon the mountains she was presenting to me. Then I felt her body move and the pleasure started to build up to a frantic desperation. I could hardly wait to discover the total oneness she'd offered, but Rita seemed determined to drive me out of my mind. Her body moved with torturous skill, teasing, taunting, but never allowed more than a voluptuous touch to build the need into a tight terrible pain that became more and more anguished.

Her arms were supporting her on each side of my head, while those incredible breasts swung back and forth under the desperate kisses I found myself pressing upon them. She was in total control and liking every moment of it.

Then suddenly I felt her shift the weight of her body, the movement of her thighs and hips changed and all at once I gasped in utter pleasure. It was so intense that I couldn't control myself any longer. I fairly went wild, mad with the passion of it all.

After what seemed an eternity, Rita's form lifted away and collapsed on the bed beside me, breathing heavily.

I was exhausted to the point where it was impossible to move. For a long time I merely lay there, unaware of anything other than the sensation of release in my body after her prolonged game of sensual teasing. A half-sleep must have settled over me, because the next thing I knew Rita was tapping my cheek with a soft hand.

"Billy, time to get up," she said.

Slowly sitting up, a little dazed, I looked up at Rita. She was fully dressed now.

"How'd you like me?" she inquired.

"You're amazing," I admitted, starting to reach for my clothing.

"You'll find all of us amazing in our own ways. But Big Rita has many more tricks." She laughed. "We'll have plenty of time to explore everything." She shrugged. "Don't want to use it all up in one day, though. I'll show you your room...or, rather, let you pick from several we have vacant."

MURDER MOST TERRIBLE! BY CHARLES NUETZEL

Chapter Four

It was about four in the afternoon by the time I'd chosen a room and got rid of Rita. Sitting on the bed, smoking a cigarette, I thought about this Castle of Eros. There was no doubt about it being a heaven for any single guy wanting one hell of a long sex orgy. But there was something nagging at my mind. All during ray hitch in the service I had wanted women like Rita and Mic—women willing to give all they had, openly, without question, no games. But now that it was happening, I could only think how degrading it all seemed. I realized what truly bothered me.

I thought of Judy, slightly built, innocent little sister, living in this place, acting like Rita and Mic—a plaything for any man they wanted to turn on. The realization made me sick.

So far I'd discovered nothing about Judy's death, other than the fact that her head had been bashed in, that she'd been with some man—or woman?—and had been naked when killed. The murderer had gotten off Scot free. It seemed amazing, yet that was it. Obviously the rule of law was out, here on Eros. And King was master of the Law book—assuming there was any. I had the feeling that this man didn't give a damn about finding out who had killed her, what had actually happened. It seemed that he'd merely gone through some mechanical actions, to appear concerned.

Rita had managed to keep my mind so totally upon her mammary glands that it had been impossible to think about Judy. A wash-out, that meeting with Rita, insofar as getting information about Judy's death. Why would anybody have killed Judy? Considering the free, open sexual atmosphere of the place, surely it couldn't have been a murder of passion or jealousy. Then why?

Tormented with such thoughts, I sat there for a whole hour, getting nowhere. When a gong sounded in the hallway, and a voice announced dinner, I stood, stubbed out the cigarette and left the room.

For the first time I got a chance to see more members of this cult of Eros.

The men were amazingly handsome, the women surprisingly beautiful, except for one tall, brown haired female who looked like an old maid teacher. As she passed me in the hall, she smiled and said:

"You're new here aren't you?"

"Just today."

"There'll be a great party later tonight," she told me, touching my shoulder with long, tapered fingers. "I'll be looking forward to meeting you totally."

Her rather plain face, took on a hauntingly lustful look, then she moved on ahead of me. Mentally I thought: The Witch of Eros!

A tall man, with sandy-reddish blonde hair, cut short, blue bright eyes, and a ruddy complexion, walked up to me and announced: "I'm Curly

Davis—everybody calls me either Curly or Buck. I rather like the Curly from the girls and Buck from the men. What's your name?"

"Bill."

He laughed. "Glad to know you, just plain Bill."

Then he reached into his shirt pocket, pulled out a pencil, said: "Speak into the mike for us—Bill. What do you think about our little place here?"

We were now walking down the staircase, and the man's grinning, friendly face and words caught on, fast. It was obvious that here was a guy who would be fun in any crowd.

"I think it's a little tame during the day, only a lot of girls."

Curly Buck laughed. "Wait until night, buddy, just wait. Say, did you ever hear about the chicken and the scrambled eggs?"

I gave him a double take. "What about them?"

"Well, the mother hen took one look at the scrambled eggs and a large tear ran down her beak as she said: Look at those crazy mixed up kids." He laughed again. "Sorta makes you all choked up, doesn't it?"

It was impossible to keep from smiling, there was something about Buck that made a guy grin. His ruddy, square face seemed perpetually cheerful.

Putting the pencil back into place, he clapped an arm around about me and said: "Hear you were a friend of Judy's."

"No, not quite. A friend of a friend. Said to look her up but Mic saw me first."

"Oh, Mike—she's swell, don't you think? Real innocent when she first came here. We fixed her up—and she matured fast. Judy was much the same.

"Now they were a lively pair. What'd you think of Mike?"

"Lovely girl," I stated, wondering whether I should admit having shared a full service delight with her.

"Great pair of tits," he remarked as we entered the main dining hail, where a large, long table was set with a lacy cloth and silver utensils. Dark wood panels covered all the walls. There were several wine glasses at each place.

"It was quite a shock hearing about Judy's death," I stated as casually as possible. "From what her friend said, she seemed like a great girl."

"Terrible. Terrible. Somebody got a little too wild, I'd say," Buck agreed.

"What do you think really happened?"

"Who knows? She played men off against one another."

"How's that?" I asked sharply.

Just then a tall, vampish, black-haired girl stepped up. She was amazingly attractive, slender with well molded breasts. Her hair was long and straight about her shoulders. Every inch of flesh that was exposed was deeply tanned. She wore stretch pants that seemed to suggest every inch of flesh, hiding little, and a form-fitting black sweater. She flashed my companion with a quick smile, then looked studiously at me.

"I'm Val, and you must be Billy. We'll be seeing a lot of each other—and tonight...oh, tonight." She winked at Buck. "See you Curly." With that she glided across the room to the end of the table.

"You sit next to Gale. A little on the plain side, but she really digs it. You'll learn." Buck grinned

40

wolfishly, leading me to a chair near the far end of the table away from Val. He seated himself opposite me.

Already the table was filling with the resident guests. The woman I'd seen in the hallway sat next to me. I felt a sense of regret, because a beautiful, full-breasted girl sat next to Curly Buck. Her generous smile greeted me with open invitation.

"I'm Kathy Sherman." She was blonde, green eyed and gave the appearance of really liking to swing. But I recognized her as one of the women I had seen in the room that afternoon, loving it up with each other,

Suddenly, under the table, I felt her naked feet reach out and touch my lap. A mischievous grin spread wide as she wiggled her toes.

"Hello, again," the brown haired girl at my left greeted, while her hand moved to my thigh, making no pretense of modesty, "We're all happy to see you. I'm Gale Hanson,"

Kathy Sherman said cattily, "She's worked as a secretary all her life. You know secretaries."

Feeling a sense of sympathy for Gale, I touched her fingers, caressing them gently. It was obvious that she wanted attention from the bright smile that spread her thin mouth over slightly uneven teeth.

Kathy Sherman laughed, "He doesn't know about secretaries, Gale, you'll have to show him all about them, I'm sure you will do everything in your power to make it *look good.*" The last was belittling, implying that it couldn't possibly be very good.

Curly Buck glared at Kathy. "Shut up! Just because you're rich and spoiled and beautiful doesn't mean you're the only woman around."

I felt Kathy's feet move up forward, their toes tickling my thighs. Suddenly I felt Gale's hand whip out, slapping at the intruding feet.

"Ouch!" Kathy cried, her face contorting. "You'll be sorry for that."

"Just keep your feet to yourself," Gale snapped, nastily, "This isn't the time to be playing footsie."

"Then what the hell were you doing?"

"Oh, shut up," Gale retorted. I waited for her hand to be return and was almost relieved when it didn't come back to my thigh.

The group quieted down after Andy King had arrived, the last to come to the table. Rita Roselanda was on his right, and a strikingly lovely black woman on his left. She was introduced as Cherry Florence. She was a large, big boned, big breasted female who would have hardened a man's hunger for female flesh even if her color had been green.

Kathy Sherman said cattily: "She's a stripper by profession—so she says, but I think she was selling it to the customers. You know these strippers!"

Sue Kong, the Japanese girl whom I had met earlier spat out at Kathy, "Can't you keep that tongue of yours quiet?"

"Girls, girls!" Andrew King cried, "We'll have no more of that."

He glared at Kathy. "Say you're sorry."

"I'm sorry, Father King." She looked honestly contrite.

"It is not the way of our people to fight among ourselves. We are the lovers, the people who see clearly that love is the beginning and end of all things. We do not want fighting in the castle of love.

Remember, my children, love is the way of life, in every act and action, every word."

Mic Corning came bouncing in late with a young man named Barney Smith. They sat on the other side of the table. I noticed that the balance of women and men was not quite equal.

The Master of Eros, Andy King, stood, raised his arms toward the ceiling. "Let us bless this table, and all those who are gathered around. Let it be a time of sharing, a time of love. Blessed be God that created all things and gave to His Children the Divine right to know true pleasure, total union, complete joy in the eating of food, the experiencing of physical desires, the ability to share oneself with others, and the mind to understand the full meaning of that sharing. Eat well. Drink of the wines as if they were gold. Food strengthens the body, wine tones it to a sharp peak, but can also dull its edge if taken in too great a quantity. Remember, the rites of love are to always follow! Be prepared for the best that life has to offer."

With that he tapped one of the wine glasses with a spoon. Immediately, houseboys came forward and served huge platefuls of roast beef, potatoes smothered in rich dark gravy, buttered carrots.

All during the meal the conversation was light, and on general topics. Then suddenly somebody brought up Judy's name. I don't quite remember who, because the wine was flowing freely, a glass being refilled immediately upon being two thirds empty.

Curly Buck was saying, "You know, the funny thing about that was she disappeared several hours before, It was after that loud pool party. I saw her take off with a couple of guys. Both from outside. Then later I saw her with Sue Kong. After a while, Judy went out to the beach, alone."

Sue piped in, saying, "She told me she was meeting some one there. She seemed worried—or pre-occupied. All day she seemed detached."

Gale Hanson added, "I think something was bothering her. What...I don't know. But it was strange. Very strange."

Father King interrupted with, "I don't see what all this talk will get us. We've gone over it a thousand times and there's no evidence to point to anybody. We were all accounted for. I think it's best we all try to forget it."

Gale stated sharply: "That's the trouble with the whole thing. We've all been willing to forget that Judy was murdered. That's serious."

Kathy catted back, "You're always making something out of nothing. It's the secretary in you. Not enough excitement in life—so you make excitement where there is none. I agree with Father King—we should forget it. There's no real evidence that Judy was murdered. She could have fallen from the cliff."

"Do you really believe that?" Gale countered in a very serious voice.

"What else is there to believe?" Kathy inquired, eyes widening. "The fact is that she's dead, and none of us would have done it."

I sat there just listening, watching the expressions of everybody sitting around the table. They all seemed innocent but indifferent. Gale Hanson seemed to be the most concerned. I wondered if there was a reason. I determined that at my first

44

chance I'd get alone with Gale and pump her on the subject. The danger lay in giving myself away. I didn't want anybody to realize my obsession about Judy, or that I really was her brother.

The topic of conversation finally changed to other subjects and dinner was finished off with choice imported cheeses.

"How do you like our place?" Kathy inquired as we were sipping coffee and brandy.

"Delightful. I never guessed that there would be such outstanding meals."

"The Master believes in loving to the hilt, both people and food. All the senses must be catered to," she told me. "I'll tell you all about it sometime." There was promise in her eyes as they flashed me a quick, sultry look.

Andy King stood suddenly, said: "It's about time to prepare for the guests. They should be arriving shortly." He looked at the wrist watch on his right arm. "In just about twenty-three minutes to be exact. Make yourselves ready, my children."

Curly Buck Davis came around to my side as we were all getting ready to leave, "Let's have another brandy in the smoker."

I readily took his invitation, following him out of the room and down the hallway to a small library room, in which a bar was pushed up against the far wall,

He immediately went to the bar. "Brandy...or something else?"

"Anything."

I gazed at the wall of books. There were countless pocket books, all published "For Adults Only." A couple of titles caught my eye. Curly Davis came up arid handed me a large brandy snifter,

"How do you like the collection?"

"Interesting."

I pulled out a book with a provocative title.

"That looks like a wild one."

"This room is devoted to soft-cover books." Buck pulled down another title, "I know the author of this one."

"Any good?"

"Not really. Nothing like the real classics. In the King's study—there is a real collection of erotica. I helped him gather some of them."

"How'd you learn about King's Eros Cult?" I inquired conversationally, after taking a sip of the brandy.

"Got to know Val. We hit it off good, and then I just came naturally into the fold," he stated, putting the book back into place. "Was in show business before that. An agent. Still have some interest there— but I got tired of the rat race, decided to live my life a little. This is certainly the place for that. I'd been married for some years—to a wife who was, in all honesty, a little frigid. We split up—I started playing around, met Val—and wound up here. The small income I get from my investments makes it possible to afford this kind of life. It's a breeze—as you can see."

He grinned a little too broadly. There was something about his manner that puzzled me.

"What did you do before you joined the Army?" he asked.

"Oh, you know about that?"

"Information gets around pretty fast. But so far the only thing we know is that you were in the

Army, had a friend who knew Judy—and learned about us. That's just about it." He peered down at me as if studying a bug.

"Your information is fairly complete. I was drafted like a lot of guys, managed to survive and got out. Regardless of what one believes about the war in South Vietnam, we're in it—and since war is hell, I'm glad to be out,"

"See much action?"

"Enough to make me want to stay out of the fighting zones. Not that I'm a coward, but I want to live."

"What is it like over there?" Curly Buck inquired, looking at me over the edge of the brandy glass.

"Hell," I said.

"Why don't we just pull out and let them have what they want? Communism is good for small countries—and it's about time we admitted it."

I shook my head. "Don't buy that. Can't. There are other means of helping them help themselves. They have a right to have a voice in what happens to their lives. How would you like Big Brother telling you what to do? No! Can't buy that."

A soft, low voice called from the doorway. "Boys do you have to talk about war?"

I turned, it was Kathy Sherman, dressed in an Empire style dress that was topless. Her breasts were beautifully shaped, just made for such a dress, firm and youthful, self supporting, their nipples nicely placed high on their oval, supple forms.

Her large green eyes were focused on me, her glance moved up and down as if they were feasting on something which highly delighted her.

"Do me a favor, Curly, get lost," she said.

Buck grinned widely, winked at me, then shrugged. "You heard what the lady said—gotta leave you to your fate."

The minute he left the room, Kathy closed and locked the door, then turned to face me, leaning against the wood panel door, breasts thrust out. Her pointed tongue moistened the sensual, full lips.

"Now, big boy, I think you and I have something of interest to converse about." Her right hand reached up and gently caressed her breasts. "I don't believe in mincing words. In a short time the Dance of Passion will bring you and Val together...that is the usual routine and I see no reason to let her be first with you."

She started forward, hips rolling. "Come, let's get to know each other...after all, we're going to be long time friends, living here together like we do. And there's nothing I like more than having the chance to know all my friends as intimately as possible."

Chapter Five

I guess there was no reason for me to feel slightly surprised at a third woman wanting to get ahead of Val.

"You are frank," I said when she had come to a stop in front of me. Her hips were almost touching mine. I could smell the scent of her perfume. She seemed to breathe sexual energy just standing there, looking up, wide-eyed, waiting for what was obviously expected of me.

"I joined the Eros cult because I like sex and I don't like being coy, I like the idea that when I want a man, all I have to do is go up to him and say, 'Let's do it.' No silly games or rules."

The temptation of her naked breasts was too much to ignore. I reached up and cupped a hand over her right breast, palming the nipple until it was hard.

"That's pretty good," she murmured, a slow smile forming on her lips. I felt the press of one thigh between my legs and all at once found it impossible to control myself.

Grabbing at her, I pulled Kathy hard against me, found her lips, which opened wide to my kiss.

A moment later, coming up for breath, I heard

her say, "Take it easy, big boy."

Then, as I reached for her again, Kathy slipped away, laughing. "Half the fun is in the chase. Bet you can't get me."

I reached out again, but she slipped away.

"I thought you didn't play games," I countered.

Her lips taunted me. Caressing her hips and then touching tapered fingers to her breasts, Kathy Sherman stood about a yard away, breathing heavily, staring up at me with burning fires in her eyes. "Come and get me, Billy. Come and get what I can give you."

I took a step forward, and she moved back the same distance. Abruptly I leaped at the small woman, grabbed she shoulders roughly, and slammed her against me. When I attempted to kiss those lips, her right hand slashed out at my face, hitting it hard.

Laughing, she glided away as I stood there stunned,

Angered to the point of losing interest, I whipped around and started toward the door. I didn't know what game she was playing, but it wasn't the kind I'd expected or cared anything about.

As my hand reached the door knob, Kathy came rushing up. Her hands embraced my hips. "Please, Billy, don't leave now...don't—I'll be good. Real good."

I turned, looked at her. She slipped to her knees, stared up at me like a little child, eyes pleading.

"Please, I want you..."

"Then why do you tease?" I demanded, still irritated, but again excited by the lovely creature below me, breasts naked to my gaze.

"I want you...I'll do anything you say. Please. Punish me for what I did. Hit me, beat me—anything you want—but don't leave me like this."

Her whole body was trembling, tears running down her cheeks. I stood there puzzled. What kind of perverse creature was this?

Slowly, Kathy came to her feet and unzipped the back of her dress, which slid down to her hips. Then she worked her way out of the dress. As I would have expected, there was nothing other than Kathy Sherman underneath.

"Please, Beat me...hit me...punish me...anything you want...but take me." Her voice was deep, husky, the words trembling past tortured lips.

Reluctantly I reached out for Kathy, and she immediately slipped away.

"Come, bet you can't get me," she challenged, hands on hips, face suddenly taunting, a half smile on her lips. The total change was startling.

But as I stood there, unmoving, Kathy's pouting, lower lip trembled, "Please, chase me. Catch me, force me. I want it so bad I could cry."

Shrugging inwardly, I decided to play it her way, just to see what would happen. There was no question that I desired Kathy. Under the circumstances no man could help it.

I rushed forward so abruptly that she seemed startled to inactivity. Then, just as I was about to reach her, that lovely body slipped away. This time I followed the woman, making a running tackle at her tapered legs. The two of us slammed down onto the carpeted floor. It was a delightful tangle of flesh that squirmed and fought under mine. Now I knew that

Kathy really wanted to be mock raped and being at the point of madness myself I was equal to the challenge.

I struggled with her, finally getting hold of both her arms and fairly slapping them to the floor. Then I lowered my head, struggling until one lovely breast was under my lips. The nipple was firm as my tongue teased it.

All at once Kathy's body went limp, a moan of pleasure came from deep within her chest. But the moment I released her arms, thinking that now she would co-operate, she twisted away, attempted to escape my kisses. Frantic to the point of desperation, I slapped out at Kathy's face.

She lay still, gazing up at me, eyes submissive. "Get undressed" she cried. "I can't stand it, can't wait."

Doing as she suggested, I watched the woman, who just lay there, looking up at me, waiting, every once in a while writhing as if unable to lie still.

When I finally was able to move down to her, Kathy rolled away, but not beyond reach.

"Damn it, stay still," I cursed, and grabbed at her.

"Yes, *make* me stay still," she pleaded, struggling to get away.

Brutally I yanked her bodily against mine and she melted at first contact. Her arms gripped mine like a vise. Her lips crushed against my lips, eager for a passionate kiss. What her hips did in the meantime was enough to drive any man crazy. Her thighs moved back and forth, teasing in such a manner that I couldn't stand it more than a few moments, Thrusting her back, arms pinned on each side of her head, I moved to join our bodies in the final plunge of passion.

"Oh, Bill, I can't let you do this...please you can't do this...I...oh, God—that felt good—good... yes...again, do it again and again and again...keep it up forever—never stop. Oh you bastard, what have you made me do...? Oh, good, good, that's so good..." She kept up a continual babble throughout the act. But when she reached the final peak, she could only gasp and claw at my back. The ultimate moment left us clinging together, spent but satisfied, I fell back against the floor.

Kathy moved close, her hand caressed me tenderly. "Oh, you were good, so good. I never felt so good… I just love the way it feels.... But I have to be convinced the man really turns on...to know my body drives him to the point where he can't control his instincts." Her hand was doing things to me and I was beginning to revive.

Then suddenly Kathy slipped over me, her body crushing close, eager, as if not able to get near enough. Her thighs teased while lips kissed.

"Oh, Billy, you turn me on…really great, just great. And I know you like *me*...I just know you like me! I can feel what you like...I can feel what I'm doing to you...oh, this is so good, so wonderful so great...I just can't help myself. I can't help myself...can't...just can't get enough...oh, gosh, golly, God...we can...can do it...again." The words gushed out like wild from her trembling lips as I felt the wonderful joy of our second union. This time it was Kathy all the way, controlling every moment, every instant of pleasure. It lasted so long I thought for a while it would never end. The final peak of pleasure lifted me upwards in a sputtering explosion and I fell back against the carpet again, hardly able to think or move.

I heard Kathy getting dressed but did not open my eyes. I just relaxed in total exhaustion. She had changed her tune.

"You dirty bastard! You turned me on. You made me do terrible things," she cursed under her breath. Then a moment later I felt her lips on mine. "But I loved it, every beautiful moment of it. You were great, lover. You made me feel great all over. We'll have to do it again—maybe tomorrow. Is that a date?"

I just looked up at her, but didn't say anything. The idea of having to make love to another woman that night seemed impossible. Just about the last thing I wanted to do.

Slowly I sat up, looked at Kathy as she moved to the door.

She hesitated, looked back at me. "Aren't you going to get dressed? We don't want the others to know what happened in here—especially Val. She'd be furious if she knew I'd gotten the first goodie from you."

I wondered how Kathy would react if she knew that two other girls had beaten her to the punch. Or did she already know? I was also beginning to wonder if it would be possible to survive long enough to get the information I wanted about my sister's death. But, while dressing, I began to think that with a little rest, a couple of drinks and the right kind of build-up, I might function during the main event with Val. I followed Kathy out into the hallway. Her swinging fanny moved casually away from me, as if nothing had happened. I wondered why she was so mixed up. She'd come at me all lust, demanding that I make love to her, then changed and played coy games. I realized it hadn't been any real reluctance, but the desire to be forced into doing something that consciously she craved, but subconsciously was feeling great guilt about. Her desire to be hit suggested that she was a masochist. The idea caused a shudder to rush through me. I'd always thought of women as something to protect, to take care of. Had my sister Judy turned into something like these other sex-obsessed women? It seemed incredible.

In a depressed mood I continued down the hallway, and was passing the study where Andrew King held his private interviews. The door was slightly open, and I decided if nobody was in there, I would nose around his study in hopes of finding some clue as to the real circumstances behind Judy's death. It seemed to me that some of the people here at the castle were a bit too casual about it. And their attitude, I was beginning to believe, had to be on King's orders. He ruled, there was no question about it, with an iron hand, despite his fatherly pose. The island was in international waters and the term King applied in more than one way to the Master of Eros. He was, also, the law—for outside of any he might enforce, there simply wasn't any law!

As I was about to step into the room, a tall, well dressed man swung the door wide and came out. He was wearing a neatly-pressed business suit that seemed so totally out of place for the Castle of Eros that I froze in surprise.

He stood there, attempting to get past me.

In the room, behind the large desk sat Andrew

King. He sprang to his feet as he saw me.

"What the hell are you doing here?" he cried, anger in his voice and on his angular features.

"I just...came by to see you," I managed to fumble out.

The man in front of me said something under his breath, darting a quick, worried look at the Lord of Eros, but in a language that I didn't understand.

"Step in here, I'll have a word with you. Obviously you don't know the rules of our society." King spoke, as if I were a small child who had been found sneaking around places he had no business investigating.

Once I'd moved aside, the suited man went down the hall. I closed the door behind me, then turned, toward Andrew King.

"I'm sorry if I interrupted something—"

"Sit down, young man. I don't know what you were doing, what you had in mind, but I must impress upon you that of all the rooms in this castle, there is only one where members are not allowed to come, without an invitation. This is the room. I have reasons for this, which, to be frank, are purely selfish." His tone of voice and manner changed from controlled anger to casual friendliness.

"I like a certain amount of privacy. When I want company—I seek it out, if I want to be alone, I come in here. I also carry on the business matters here." Finally he sat down, in the chair which creaked under his weight.

"Now, tell me, what was it you wanted to see me about?" he added.

Doing a quick ad-lib, I said, "Well, I was in the pocket book library—Buck said that your hardcover collection is in this room. I was interested in browsing through it and—"

King seemed relieved, though it was hard to tell, under the bushy length of beard and long white hair.

"Well, now, my boy, I can't say that I blame you. I'll make you a promise: Sometime during the week I'll show you this collection, Right now we must prepare for the party. I'll explain what is going to happen."

He stood, came close, put a friendly arm about my shoulders. "First will come the gathering, when the people will he able to see one another, select those who interest them. Then come the drums and the Dance of Passion. I believe you will like what Val has planned for tonight. After that, the excitement will have built up so much that everybody will be ready to begin the real activities." We passed through the doors, and King took out a large key and locked them. "Private collections can be scattered among many homes—if loaned to the casual membership. We find it necessary to keep it under lock and key."

He led the way down the hall toward the huge room of the Roman Orgy walls, with the round bed in its center.

"Now, remember, the guests are people anxious to learn the full meaning of total free union—the complete joining of spirit. The ones who attract you and feel are free to give totally of themselves, grab 'em and enjoy; this is what they are here for. Some will be shy—it will be your duty to make things easy for them.

"I realize you are new here, but in time you will be like us of the inner circle. We're the love children. All they want is to be needed, to be wanted, to live as nature intended. The night is young, the weekend just beginning. Meals will not be served at regular hours—food is spread out in different parts of the living quarters—help yourself to all the drink and food you desire. Make yourself at home. All weekend this will be a place of total sharing. It is a great time for a new member to join us, for by Monday you will be very much like the rest of us."

With that he led me into the meeting room. The lights were dimmed, while flickering flames cast dancing shadows upon the wall. Incense burned. The buzz of conversation was low. The place was crowded with nude and half-nude men and woman, lounging on throw rugs around the center dais, upon which Val King lay, seeming unaware of all about her, as if blinded. It took me only a moment to real-ize that the woman was doped in some manner. But her eyes turned at our entrance and a bright fire lighted in them as they met mine. There was no doubt about it. Val had picked me as her target to-night.

Chapter Six

Drums were beating hypnotically, and the flickering flames of half-a-dozen torches cast shadows and sharp high-lights across the dim room. There was a savage, pagan atmosphere in the air itself, accented by the erotic scent of the incense which, together with the torches, filled the room with smoky haze. Where the drums came from was anybody's guess: probably speakers were hidden behind curtains or set in the walls.

The men and women sat on rugs, alone and in pairs. Some were totally naked, others wore nothing but strings and cloth like jungle savages or pagan worshippers from the past. There must have been at least fifty people here, almost equally divided between male and female. As the drumbeats grew louder and faster, several couples began intimate sexual play. A couple to my right was totally taken up by one another. The fact that they were both men attracted no attention. They were unselfconscious as two flies mating in mid-flight. To the far side of the dais I could see two women standing, locked in a passionate embrace, breasts cushioned against one another. One woman was fat to the point of repulsiveness, the other slender as a palm tree. They slowly slipped down, still locked in each other's arms. The dais and Val King blocked my view of their further activities.

I rested my eyes on Val, who was swathed in fine silks that covered her hips and breasts completely. Lacy netting fluffed about her body from ankle to neck.

I found myself scanning the room for the man who had been dressed in the business suit. But if he was here, he had removed it.

My eyes rested upon a man and woman just a short distance away. The woman sat upright while the man bent over to kiss her heavy breasts. Neither was outstandingly attractive, though hardly repulsive.

A soft hand reached out and touched my shoulder. I'd removed my shirt, feeling out of place among all the nudity. I turned, looked into the eyes of an attractive young woman.

"Hello," she breathed, "You seem so alone. Mind if I join you?"

She slipped onto my throw-rug, placed a soft hand on my chest. I studied her for a moment. Her hips were broad, though her stomach was fairly flat. An otherwise perfectly-shaped body was marred by heavy thighs—but her eyes, large and eager, seemed to hold the promise of love.

"Are you a casual?" she inquired, petting my shoulder, squeezing delicate fingers against hard muscles, "I haven't seen you here before." She was moving even closer.

"Just joined, today," I admitted, looking past her shoulder toward Val, who had suddenly become aware of her surroundings. Those glazed eyes had taken on a furious interest in what I was doing.

"Oh, no wonder!" my neighbor said as she edged closer, her arms sliding around my chest. She cushioned her breasts against me. They were soft, warm and the nipples were tightening. "I'm Connie. What's your name?"

"What difference does it make?"

"Well, I don't want to do it with a *total* stranger. I like to know who gives me a thrill."

Connie automatically expected that since she was in my arms I would make love to her. The idea was attractive, though I doubted that I could do anything in such a public gathering. But everybody else seemed to accept such activity as the norm, hardly paying any attention to what other couples were doing, being too involved in their own interests. Though I *had* noticed some who seemed quite satisfied by just watching others—as if this was some kind of thrill to them; but oddly enough watching really didn't excite me.

"Name is Bill," I told Connie.

"I work as a waitress," she said. "Men are always kidding you and making passes...but their crude offers just don't interest me under *those* circumstances. That's what I like about this place. You can be yourself, because everything is reversed here at Eros. What is moral elsewhere is immoral here. It would be wrong not to offer yourself—not to take love where you find it. Out *there—a* girl is called a tramp for just wanting the human things in life."

"Well, why don't you join?" I suggested, finding it impossible to keep from fondling one of her well-formed breasts.

"I've thought about it. It's one thing to have a

fling once in a while, but I don't think I could just live here and do nothing else. You have to have contrasts in life. How much sex can a girl take in a lifetime? I live a very moral life most of the time— and come out here once a month and live it up— and nobody knows the difference."

"Don't you have any boyfriends?"

"Yes, one I like very much. But I wouldn't *think* of letting him have me. He'd think I was promiscuous. But a girl has feelings like men. I like to do it. I like to know the feel of a man. My fingers just love the feel of a man. But you can't admit that to most of the guys you know."

The drums were now beating so loud that it was almost impossible to hear her words. She leaned closer, and our lips touched. Her mouth was wide open under the kiss and I felt the point of a tongue search up through my mouth. She tensed all over and her finger-nails dug deep into my back.

All of a sudden it didn't matter if a million eyes were upon us. The only two people alive were myself and this Connie, the waitress who lived a moral life—most of the time.

Suddenly the drums were silent. It was stunning.

Connie pushed me away.

"Damn," she said, "Just when things were getting interesting!"

She moved back to her own rug, just a few feet from mine.

All eyes now turned to Val King, who stood, frozen in one position, like a statue, arms at her side, gazing straight ahead.

A shadowy form loomed behind her, then moved to her side. It was Andy King, Lord of Eros.

62

"Oh, beloved members of our fine gathering, know that the eyes of the gods look down upon us and bless all our thoughts, all our acts which will follow, for we are the true children of nature who are aware of the meaning of life. We know that to give, to share our flesh with others is to be divine. We reach to the heavens with outstretched arms, crying, bless us, oh Eros, let us join, with each other, let us share the heavenly pleasures that are ours for the giving and receiving. The giver is the receiver, the receiver is the giver. Blessed be all of us who are fully aware of this truth of nature."

His hands reached toward the high ceiling. "Oh, divine Eros, give us your blessings, so that we may seek and discover the true meaning of life in these few hours of total sharing. We who seek you out as children of love become the holy ones. We who seek the complete pleasures that nature has offered us, are blessed with your divine passion. Love is the answer to all human problems. There is no sin other than refusal to love—to blind ourselves with ignorance of our true nature. Bless us, oh, Eros, and bless this Priestess of Love, who will dance in your honor and pick from among those present one to honor you, through the complete worship of her flesh. In the complete giving and receiving of love, she honors you, oh, Eros."

For a moment he hesitated, then dropping his hands, as a leader might give the down-beat to a group of musicians, he disappeared behind the curtain as the sound of soft, rhythmic drums swelled up again in the background.

Val's body was slowly swaying to the increasingly loud drum-beat. She moved subtly back and

63

forth, like a statue coming to life during a thunder storm.

A cold chill rushed through me, followed by a hot flash of anticipation. Everybody had said that Val would pick me as her mate for this evening. The idea, having been so many times implanted in my mind, now became a tremendous excitement.

She was lovely, tall, and graceful. Her long black hair fell straight over the netted shoulders. She had a voluptuous figure and tanned skin that almost looked bronze. She was well over five feet six inches and gave the appearance of being even taller. The shape of her breasts was sharply accentuated by the silk wrappings that held them high and bulging, their points showed through the cloth.

The drum beat grew slowly in volume and speed and Val's body started swaying more violently. Her hands began to slip up and down those long, firm thighs. Every muscle in the woman's body grew tense.

As the drums grew louder and louder, her hands crept upwards from her hips to her waist, and moved cross-wise up to the points of those breasts, finally to embrace each with an open palm.

I felt a hand touch my shoulder. It was Connie. The physical contact was startlingly sharp; electrically thrilling.

My nerves were tingling with blazing desire that had not seemed possible after the preliminary sessions but I wasn't sure whether I wanted Val or Connie most.

Connie's fingers played along my arm, then down to my thigh.

The dancer raised her hands above those gor-

geous breasts and then high above her head. A rolling action of her hips took up the rhythmic beat of
the drums with jerking motions. The drums
throbbed even louder, rocking the room with their
violence. Now, Val lowered her arms and they
peeled off the filmy outer layer of netting, leaving
her body with only the silken wrappings. She was
jerking wildly to the tempo of the drums. Her hands
caressed faster and faster over her body, first on
thighs, then hips, stomach, up to her breasts. The
dance was becoming more and more erotically exciting with every beat.

Val threw her head forward, doubling over,
hands behind her back. Then with another new series of jerks, she leaped upright, the top piece of silk
unwinding, exposing her breasts, the nipples were
hardened points against subtly rounded curves that
were perfect in shape. With arms high above her
head she trembled, jerking her hips back and forth.
A soft moan escaped her lush, full lips, the sound
growing louder and louder until it was a scream.

Connie's arms slipped about my back, and I felt
her breasts cushion against my bare back. She
crushed herself close, then her lips teased my ear-
lobe.

But my eyes were feasting upon Val as her hips
started jerking up and down, almost vibrating. The
action was highly stimulating to watch, especially
with another female pressing so tightly to my back.

Val's breasts were bouncing up and down with
every action of her tall body. The drum beats became faster and faster, her movement taking on a
quaking vibration which built so wildly that the audience was hypnotized by the sight.

Connie's fingers caressed down across my stomach and then started lower in an erotic search that came to a stop as the drums fell silent.

Val suddenly leaped from the dais, running among the audience. She moved like some graceful deer, pausing momentarily in front of different men, considering each of them, only to move on, circling twice about the big room.

Then all at once she turned and cut across the room, directly towards me.

Val came to a stop in front of me, standing totally still. The dance of passion had come to an end, and everybody in the room realized that Val had picked her mate. Connie seemed to melt away.

Val slowly reached out her hands toward me, palms up. "Come," she murmured, huskily, "You are the Chosen One."

Like a zombie I stood up finding it hard to move. Was I expected to make love to her in full view of every eye in the room?

She took my hands and gracefully glided up to the dais, pulling me after her.

"My Chosen One," she cried to the audience.

They applauded, and somewhat to my relief, Val led me forward, off the dais and across the room to a curtained doorway.

Chapter Seven

The room in which I found myself with Val King was small, with a king-size bed centered in it, leaving almost no room to walk around. Drapes hung from a canopy above the bed, made of shimmering see-through gauze. Once inside the room there was no place to go but on the bed.

Val kicked the door closed. She turned and came into my arms without word. Her body was damp with sweat, her lips salty and moist. I felt the soft, velvet flesh tremble as it met mine. Her tongue had taken up the rhythm of the dance of passion. It seemed as if the girl were possessed by some demon from Hell, totally convulsed in a screaming need that no human male could possibly appease.

It was like making love to an automated creature gone wild. Her hands directed the course of action, stripping my body bare. Her lips followed the example of those trembling hands, finding secret places of excitement that I had never realized existed before. I was drawn down into a pit of animal lust. My nerves tensed until they wanted to explode me apart.

There was no subtle building up of petting caresses, for the dance of passion had accomplished our mutual arousal long before then. Her gestures and kisses were merely a sexual rite directing our bodies toward the ultimate goal of immediate union.

I was making love, through a dizzy haze—but my awareness was pinpointed to a fiery peak of *need.*

She clasped my hands, our fingers interlocking in a tight grasp as she lowered herself backwards, doing a back bend, her feet braced solidly on the floor. That delicious body, totally naked, trembled, in anticipation of the final union. Her eyes were like those of a wild animal, lustful, almost insane with erotic desire.

As Val's back bent in an arch we became one, in a smooth operation like two parts of a machine sliding together. Pleasure laced its way up through my nervous system like a wave of electrical power, surging into my brain. Then the pistons of our hips began a slowly building movement, controlled by the woman's body as she dragged me further and further down upon the bed, not once losing the contact that made us one complete unit.

I had never experienced anything quite like this, and never have since. For the first time my whole being was engulfed, submerged by the very perfection of this moment. I felt that this was what my body had been made for; nothing more.

Val continued to move, her hips driving us faster and faster towards the ultimate goal, yet it was possible to control the final eruption of pleasure. Both of us were fully enjoying the union without guilt, without thoughts. Pure sensual pleasure submerged all other awareness.

I became aware of Val's heavy breathing, the

gasps and convulsions of approaching ecstasy. Her breasts were heaving up and down in rhythm with the trusting machinery of her hips. Then the parts of this automated sexual machine seemed to go insane, wild. Her head thrashed back and forth, low animal sounds came from tortured lips. The tension built, my senses failed one at a time, first sight, then sound, smell, leaving only the feeling of Val, who held me with every muscle in her body. We were motionless for a long, delicious moment as our sensations peaked in the final erotic finish. It seemed it had taken forever to reach that ultimate instant of time.

How long we clung to one another before Val moved, I don't know. I expected no more for she had seemed completely spent out by our first climax after the exertions of her dance. But I had much to learn about Eros and Val.

She rolled me over, and her hands began moving over my body as if she wanted to feel every inch of the lover who had given her pleasure. Her lips found mine, her tongue penetrated deep, and I felt the pressure of soft, hot thighs teasing along mine. Hands caressed my cheek, neck, shoulders. Then her lips followed the caress, her tongue making a damp trail of fire across my torso.

I felt as if I'd been plunged deep into a well from which there was no escape—even if I had wanted to find an exit. Val seemed bent on exploring all forms of pleasure with the man she had chosen as her mate.

Though I had doubted my own ability to continue her little game I felt her caressing fingers discover the trigger device that began to arouse me again. Then the fingers were replaced by soft warm lips and a knowing tongue that completed the arousal.

A warm breast met my lips, and I responded with erotic stimulation of my own. Her hips teased, tortured, played out a game that was meant to drive me over the line of sanity once more.

Like a crazed creature I grabbed at her, unable to lie there, responding helplessly to this wanton who enjoyed driving men mad. My whole being screamed to be captured by her and to capture. I wanted to be her slave and master at the same time.

With a moan of delight, she moved over me and her hips lowered as my rigid flesh found its natural home. We united as if glued together, as if fused into one complete part. Again and again she let her weight down, only to bounce away. But each re-bound was timed, faster until finally she settled, trembling convulsively, out of control, barely able to keep up-right. And then all at once we both were driven beyond control.

It seemed that we were racing into orbit in a sensual fantasy of space flight, but Val, was not sat-isfied with merely going into orbit, she wanted to explore the moon, Mars, Venus, Mercury, and fi-nally plunge us into the burning flames of the sun itself.

Towards the end of our flight there came into awareness an eagerness to make this last, final plunge into self destruction. Being engulfed by the deadly flames of the sun seemed a wonderful relief from the exhaustive torture of our trip. My body hurt all over. The miracle was that we both some-how survived, glancing off the surface of this blazing star and bouncing back into black space, only to fall in total silence onto the king-size bed in the castle of Eros.

MURDER MOST TERRIBLE! BY CHARLES NUETZEL

Chapter Eight

I felt as if my body had been pushed through a straw. Every muscle was exhausted. For a long time I merely lay there on the soft mattress of the large bed, amazed at the fantastic abilities of my body.

I'd never before been the type who could go from one woman to another during the same day, never failing. My idea of a wild weekend romance had been going to Las Vegas with some girl, checking into a room, making love, having a few drinks, doing a little gambling, having a dinner and then retiring for another bed session. In the morning if the mood struck, another bed-time party—then up for breakfast, hours of gambling, lunch, more gambling, back to the room for rest and fun and games, then up for dinner and a show and more gambling. Retire and love and sleep.

But at the castle of Eros I'd already, in one day and evening, made love to Mic, a cute little head, Rita, a hefty, aggressive Latin, Kathy, a girl who seemed to want to be punished for enjoying sexual games, and then to Val, a Goddess of Passion who seemed able to accomplish miracles in bed. Val had left, but there was no disappointment. Being alone suddenly seemed heaven. For some time I lay there, enjoying solitude fully. Then I became aware of a sound of merriment from the other room, the murmuring of laughing voices, screams of delight, running feet. It sounded like one wild party going on in the castle.

I could use a drink and a little food. I gathered up my pants and slipped into them, then stepped out into the large room beyond, which was still lighted only by the flickering torches. The sight was orgiastic. Several couples were on the floor, enjoying themselves totally. A man and woman stood in one corner, sipping drinks, talking, both nude. To my left I saw two women locked in a body embrace, lips clinging hungrily. One man and woman were taking turns chasing each other. Outside in the hallway came the sound of laughter, then a shout of surprise followed by some passionate curse of delight from the same voice.

Trying to ignore all this, I started across the room. Sharing physical love with a woman was one thing but watching others doing the same was another. As I stepped into the hall, I saw a couple of girls going at each other full blast and a man and woman standing a short distance away, intently watching. The woman was naked from the waist up, and the man kept his arm about her, fingers fondling one breast. As I passed them, I heard the woman say, "It's rather interesting the way the blonde works...did you notice the way she..."

I didn't catch the rest because two people rushed out of a room, almost knocking me over. A huge dark skinned woman, whom I immediately recognized as Cherry Florence, totally naked, was chasing a man, half naked. They were yelling at each other but neither was angry. Obviously they were having the time of their lives. When Cherry suddenly caught up with the man she pressed him against the wall, towering over him like some female demon, her dark breasts almost flush with his face.

I turned away and started down the hall, pausing at the door that led to Andrew King's private study. I had a compulsive desire to find a way into that room. I wondered about the mysterious man in the business suit. Too many pieces of information about Judy's violent death were missing. There was something going on at Eros that was not obvious on the surface.

All I really knew was that Judy had died on the beach, her head bashed in, and nobody seemed interested enough to discover what had happened. Gale Hanson seemed to suspect something—or at least she had indicated that she didn't share the attitude of the other guests about Judy's death. It seemed significant that Andrew King had been highly annoyed because I happened to see the man who had been visiting him.

I moved on down the hallway, toward another room, with double doors wide open. Soft music floated from inside and I saw a couple standing in front of a home bar. The fact that they were dressed intrigued me, so I stepped inside to discover several other decently dressed people sitting around, listening to the music, and not sharing the wild sex games going on elsewhere. The lighting was dim, much like that of a cocktail bar. A buffet table was spread with platters of canapés, dips, and snacks.

Making my way to the bar, I noticed that Sue Kong was sitting in the corner by herself. She was a dainty Oriental woman who seemed shy and yet friendly. When her eyes met mine, she smiled.

"Want a drink?" I inquired.

She nodded and I pointed to a bottle of Scotch. Her shrug indicated indifference either way.

I felt a sense of pleasure at sitting down next to Sue Kong. She was almost the only woman in the Inner Circle who had not thrown herself boldly at me.

"How come you're all by yourself?" I asked Sue.

"I think there is a time and place for everything," Sue replied in a soft, musical voice.

"I thought the Eros castle was *the place* for amorous dalliance," I said. I sipped the Scotch and studied Sue. Her black hair was piled high on her head. There was only a little makeup on that delicate, oval face. Her features were strikingly Oriental. She had slanted eyes, large and hauntingly dark; yet the accent was that of an American-born girl. She seemed not much over sixteen from her barely nubile body. Her breasts pressed against her sweater like small twins. She was so delicate it seemed as if she might shatter if touched.

"Yes, but people need to relax, too. This will go on all night, all day and night tomorrow and finally slow down Sunday afternoon."

Sue smiled up at me like a shy little girl. "Don't get me wrong," she added. "I joined because I wanted to try this kind of thing—but some of the guests drive themselves too long, and too hard. Other things are part of living, too. I like walking along the beach—enjoying the night breeze." Suddenly she stood. "Would you like to join me?"

The idea was highly appealing and I jumped at the chance, welcoming this escape from the madness of Eros.

We left the room, carrying the Scotches. She moved close to my side, but did not even take my arm.

Sue said, "I guess you think we are terrible creatures—"

"What makes you say that?" I asked.

"Well...about Judy. I noticed that you seemed quite concerned about her in the conversation at dinner tonight. Several times your face showed emotion." She reached out and touched me, for the first time, her small fingers closing around mine.

"Come—this way," she said. We had entered the hall and now she led me into another room, where a couple was locked in a burning embrace. Ignoring them, Sue Kong took me to the double glass doors, slid one open and stepped outside.

We were standing on the cemented patio outside, near a large pool with steps all around like a huge Roman bath. Sue led the way around the pool and then back through a large archway. The sound of waves was peaceful after the yells of drunken men and women in the castle of Eros.

It seemed as if Sue and I were the only people on the island as we made our way along a small stone pathway between rows of flowers.

"This is the Path of Flowers," Sue told me, picking a rose and putting it in her hair. "The Master of Eros Castle has done a beautiful job of landscaping. Everything is done with taste. Come, this way— through the brush...a shortcut."

The cool night air chilled my naked chest, and

suddenly I wished I had on my shirt. Finally we came to a grassy area which stopped short at the edge of a cliff. The moon was high, full, but clouds sometimes hid its rounded shape. Sue showed me a little stone stairway that led down the face of the bluff to the beach below.

We reached the bottom of the stairs and stepped down onto the sandy beach. It was a small, rock enclosed cove. The beach swells were gentle with lacy foam on their caps. There was a moon-path on the water.

"We really cared about Judy. She was liked by everyone. Her death seems unreal. How can you accept the passing of your love-mates? We all felt a little guilty because none of us were with her."

Sue kicked off her shoes, saying, "You don't mind if I wade in the water? I love the beach at night—it seems as if the ocean washes away the taint of Eros. My father would have a heart attack if he knew what kind of life I have been living. He still believes in the customs of old China. He would be terribly hurt. But what's a girl supposed to do in times like these? War looms over our heads more terribly than ever before in the history of Man. Why can't people just learn to live and love and forget everything else? That is really the reason for escaping to this island—things are so simple in the world of Eros."

"If only everything could be that simple, Sue!" I said, touched by some child-like quality about this woman who must be far from innocent. How misleading physical appearances can be!

It seemed she intended to do more than merely wade in the ocean. Sue Kong pulled off her sweater and then unhooked her bra. She slipped out of her skirt, stockings, and garter belt and then danced down to the water. It all came about so fast that I had merely watched the unexpected strip. She was beautifully dainty. Her breasts were well formed, though small, and their up-sweeping points were sharp. Her waist, hips, and thighs were graceful though slight. She splashed in the water, turned, laughed and called out, "Why don't you join me?"

There was such innocent delight in her voice that I could not read any sexual connotation in her invitation. She was obviously looking forward to a midnight swim, nothing more. She seemed a child of Nature, unrestrained by civilized conventions about swim suits. She was not at all self-conscious about being naked in front of a man she hardly knew.

I followed her example and ran to her side. We held hands while our feet splashed in the chilly water.

"How can you take it?" I inquired, shivering.

"You get used to it, after a while," she said "Isn't this *fun!*"

She laughed happily. "You know, Bill, you seem different from the rest—you don't exactly fit."

"How's that?"

"Oh, I don't know. You're the first man I've taken a swim with like this. I thought you might like this. You seem more sensitive than the rest." Sue frowned. "You know, there was only one other person I went swimming with—Judy. She liked to swim nude in the middle of the night, too. We were so gay. I can't believe she's gone."

That word "gay" sent a cold emotional chill

through me. "Just what kind of gay time do you mean?"

"Not the kind that word *gay* could imply. I never went in for the Lez bit, and neither did Judy. I don't know—sometimes I think maybe there is something wrong with me."

"What do you mean?"

"Because I don't like this way-out stuff. Do we *have* to talk about it?" She shook her head vigorously from side to side. "In fact, we *won't* talk about it. I refuse to."

"What would you like to talk about?"

"Nothing—let's just enjoy ourselves."

She pulled me deeper into the surf. The water chilled my knees, now. She was up to her hips in icy waves, which splashed us one after another.

All at once I seemed to be at peace with the world. As the water moved about me, it was like Sue said—I felt washed clean of the taint of Eros. I needed that, after having sex with one brazen woman after another. Of course I had enjoyed myself, but the appetite for sex without love is soon satiated. My emotions had not been touched by any of these women. I felt no sense of tenderness as I'd taken each female body in a sexual embrace.

It is possible for a man to pick up some strange woman, have cocktails, conversation, take her to a hotel room, and convince himself that he feels something more than sexual desire—for the moment. That was better than the direct-action sex of Eros, for my taste.

Yet I knew it would be possible to make love to Sue Kong in an emotional way. She was different. We could have fun together like two normal, healthy young people. Just plain fun, splashing in the surf, laughing, holding hands, aware of one another, but not unduly aroused by the fact that we were both naked; it didn't matter.

"Sue," I said, suddenly feeling a wave of protective concern for her, "How the hell did you get mixed up in this thing?"

She stopped hopping about in the water, turned and faced me, her features hidden in shadow. Then she turned her head and the moonlight glinted on her white, even teeth.

"You know, Bill, I'm not quite sure. Come to think of it. I...well, learned about sex at an early age—and found it was a lot of fun. Later...well, working as a cocktail waitress—against my father's wishes, I might add—there were many men who tried to make the scene with me—and to be honest I found myself taking up with those who appealed to *me*. I met a guy who used to come here a lot. When he discovered how much 1 liked sex he suggested I come out here some time.

"I was a little surprised to hear there was such a place. But it intrigued me. My home-life was very sheltered—very strict. I guess the idea of total freedom to be what you are and to be accepted, regardless, appealed to me. We came here one weekend and well, the next week I joined up—decided to stay on. During the week I go to work on the mainland."

After a moment of thought, she asked: "Why did you want to know?"

"Just interested. You don't seem like the others."

"I'm not. Nobody is the same. Everybody is different. The others really aren't like each other, either. But I think I know what you mean."

We were at arm's length and now Sue started to move a little closer. "Kiss me, Bill. Soft, tenderly."

Her slender arms slipped about my waist and her lips lifted up under mine. By bending my head far down, it was just possible to reach her mouth. The kiss was very tender and sweet, rather than passionate. Our bodies hardly touched.

Just as we broke the kiss a wave splashed over our bodies, almost knocking Sue over. I grabbed at her, then suddenly picked her up bodily, lifting that light form into my arms.

I knew now that I would make love to Sue, but in a lovely, sweet and romantic manner like a man who really cares and wants to give pleasure to his beloved rather than merely to satisfy his own lusts.

As I started for the shore, her arms circled about my neck, head leaning against my shoulder and neck, the sound of voices drifted across the beach to us.

I paused, startled. What instinct caused me to seek cover I'll never know. Maybe just because we were two lovers alone on a deserted beach, and the sound of others approaching seemed to violate our privacy.

My eyes searched for a hiding place and I saw some rocks half submerged in the water. Quickly making my way to them, I kept their jagged shape between us and the shore.

Sue looked at me in alarm. "What's wrong?" she whispered.

"Somebody's coming."

"There's nothing wrong with that," she pointed out, "but I do wish they would leave us alone for a while."

"Let's be quiet."

"Why hide?" she inquired, still puzzled by my attitude.

"Please, just a little game, for fun. I don't want them to know we are here." I now recognized the voices of two men—but I could not understand the words, spoken in that strange language I'd heard outside Andrew King's office earlier that evening.

Sue shivered.

We were submerged to our waists, holding onto the rocks that hid us from the shore. I peeked over the edge of the rock and saw two shadowy forms standing on the sand, animatedly talking.

"It's Curly," Sue whispered.

The other was dressed in a business suit and I was sure it was the same man I'd seen coming out of King's office.

Suddenly the man Sue had recognized as Curly Buck Davis took a swing at the other, who quickly ducked under the blow, reached into his coat pocket and pulled out something that flashed in the moonlight.

Sue stifled a cry of alarm and I had an impulse to rush out of the water and stop the fight. But before I could do anything, the suited man plunged the knife forward, deep into Curly's chest. He slumped slowly to the sand, on his knees, then fell forward, face down.

MURDER MOST TERRIBLE! BY CHARLES NUETZEL

Chapter Nine

Sue Kong clung to me, sobbing like a frightened child. I watched, stunned by the scene before us. The thought of what might happen if the man discovered we were watching, kept me very quiet and still.

It had all happened so quickly, without warning, that I still could not believe it.

The suited man leaned down, rolled Curly over, pulled out the knife and, after a moment, stood upright. He turned in our direction and for a second I feared we had been discovered. But apparently he was merely staring out over the ocean, blankly. The man turned and half ran up the stone stairs toward the house. When he had disappeared, I pulled Sue upright.

"Come, quick."

She followed obediently.

Fortunately the man hadn't seen our clothing on the sand. It was dark and he had been totally taken up in his own drama.

I rushed out of the water and to Curly's side. Looking down at the still form, I tried to convince myself this was only some fantastic nightmare.

Blood was slowly covering his chest where the

knife had been plunged and then pulled away.

I leaned close, searched for some sign of life, but there was no heartbeat. He was quite dead.

Sue was standing at my side, trembling with terror.

"We...better get out of here," I urged, grabbing her hand. "Come. Get your clothes. Hurry."

Something warned me that the faster we made our way back to the house the better it would be for both of us. There was little doubt in my mind that if the other man discovered we'd seen him kill Curly, our own lives would be in danger.

"Bill, what...are...we...going to do?" Sue was sobbing.

"Come...I'll explain later." I started gathering our clothing. "Hurry. We have to get away from here—fast."

"We have...to tell Andy King." She looked up at me, lips compressed stubbornly.

"No. I'll explain later."

I half dragged her across the beach. "Is there any other way out of here?"

Sue nodded. She pointed to our left. There was an opening in the rocks that surrounded this sandy cove and I made my way toward it, pulling Sue after me.

In silence we slipped through the opening and then up a sharply cut ledge-like path that made its way up to the top of the rocky cliffs. Once we were on top, I surveyed our surroundings as the moon came out from behind a cloud. The Castle of Eros was some hundred yards away, surrounded by thick trees that stood up against the night sky like black beings from some fantastic world. Brush and grass grew high around us. This part of the island had been allowed to remain natural, untouched by man.

"Can we get into the house from this direction, without anybody knowing that we came from the beach?" I asked, starting to sort our clothing.

"Yes," she answered in a small voice. She was still terrified and puzzled. As I handed over her clothing, Sue began dressing automatically. "We have to...tell...somebody."

"Look, Sue. I don't know what's going on here, but that man was in King's office this evening, and take my word for it—there is some connection. We'd better remain silent about this."

She nodded, then pulled on her sweater.

Fully dressed, she led the way through thickly matted brush until we were just outside the southern wing of the Castle of Eros. The night had turned suddenly colder. A strong breeze cut across the island, carrying the laughing, gay voices from the castle to our ears.

"We have to...go in the side entrance." Sue paused. "Wait," she said.

In a swift movement she removed her sweater, then the bra. She let down her hair and mussed it up. "We have to look like...lovers."

Then Sue led the way to a side door, which easily opened when I turned the doorknob. Beyond was darkness I heard distant laughter and gay voices.

"Come with me...we'll go to my room," she whispered, squeezing my hand almost to the hurting point.

As we moved forward I thought how strangely things had developed. Before I'd been totally alone in my search for Judy's murderer, and now I had a companion, as well as a suspect.

We made our way across the central hall, where half a dozen couples were engaged either in conversation or embraces. Sue led me up the stairs and then down the hall to a room on the west wing of the house.

Once we had closed the door behind us, she came into my arms, trembling. Soft sobs were shaking her frail frame. The intimacy of our situation did not arouse me—I was thinking of the jarring implication of the murder. I could feel Sue's breasts, naked and warm against my flesh, yet I felt no surge of passion, but rather experienced a great wave of protectiveness.

Holding Sue close, I said: "Take it easy...it is all right. Sue...take it easy."

Slowly the sobs came to an end, but she continued to cling to me like a helpless, frightened child.

"What...what are we going to do?" she whispered in a shaky voice, her face looking up at me.

"Nothing—right now. Wait."

"Shouldn't we tell...somebody? The authorities should be informed and—"

"What authorities?"

"*The* authorities. A murder just took place!" she insisted stubbornly.

"There aren't any authorities out here. Other than Andrew King, this is not the United States. And I don't believe King would...I just don't know." I held her at arm's distance, studied that oval face for a moment, then asked: "Can you just do me this favor?—wait. Wait until we see what happens. Maybe somebody else will report the body—and if things look right, I'll tell Andy King exactly what we saw. Okay?"

She nodded, tight-lipped. Then Sue moved away, sat on the bed with her hands in her lap, looking like a frightened little child.

"Tell me everything you know about this place," I suggested.

"There's not much to tell, except what you have seen. We live here—and there is free love every day and night. We have parties like this at least once a month—sometimes special parties."

"Any foreigners?"

She seemed startled by the question.

"There have been...come to think of it...a couple of times—three since I've been here—we've had special parties for...foreign clubs, Andy called them. I never discovered what country they came from though." Her pretty face squinted in thought. "Come to think of it, they *were* rather odd parties. I mean, a little different. We had a lot of drinks beforehand, and then each of us here was paired off...with one of the guests. It was a little more formal than these...gatherings like tonight. It never occurred to me to question...we never question anything the Master of Eros suggests. He makes some kind of explanation and we accept it. But there have been some strange activities surrounding these parties. Andy instructed us each time to keep the guests happy and busy—but not to let them go out on the beach. The pool and immediate area surrounding the building was on limits."

She paused, looked up at me with an odd expression on her dainty face. "You know...I was never alone at such times. Always had one of the guests at my side. Usually we stayed in the house—

eating, drinking, having a gay time of it, but I don't think anybody went outside. This would go on for several days and nights. It's funny that nobody ever thought it strange."

I was beginning to develop a theory about why everybody at Eros was being so blinded to logic: they were living a wild, sensual life, free of moral restraints. They were happy about it and, being half-drunk much of the time, they did not even consider questioning the authority of the Master of Eros.

Then Sue Kong dropped the clincher: "You know, Bill, it was during one of these special parties that...Judy was killed."

Chapter Ten

The two of us stayed in her room the rest of the night. Sue was cuddled in my arms, sleeping, but tired as I was, my own thoughts kept me awake, running around and around in a dizzy whirl. We had talked for a long time, until exhaustion had over-whelmed her.

I tried to reconstruct the circumstances of Judy's death. Apparently she had broken the rule about go-ing outside—why, was unimportant in itself. Yet she had apparently been able to get away with it. Then she'd been murdered. Andy King had ques-tioned everybody at the Castle, and discovered they were all accounted for.

The man in the business suit who had killed Curly Davis spoke a foreign language—during cer-tain parties, foreign people had come to the castle and nobody was supposed to go outside. On the sur-face it had seemed a rule for the guests; but I was beginning to believe it was to keep the members of the cult from going outside. Why?

As dawn started brightening the eastern horizon, I slipped away from Sue, who stirred slightly, but did not awaken; then went to the dresser for a pack of cigarettes. Taking one from the pack, I lighted it nervously, moved to the window, looking out across the Pacific Ocean.

All at once everything about Eros disgusted me. There was the smell of intrigue, but what kind was hard to figure out with the limited information I now possessed.

This island off the coast of California, beyond the control of U.S. authorities was an ideal setting for intrigue. The society, cult, sex club, lived in a state of non-thinking sexual pleasure, and therefore accepted all that the Lord and Master of Eros dictated, without question. Andy King had fixed his authority with a double-talk that sounded much like religion. Yet some of the members had a sense of guilt. No love entered the relationships—only a lot of sexual madness. They all indulged in food and drink and sex in unlimited amounts, staying on the physical and sensual level so there wasn't time or energy to question what might really be going on here.

Judy had been killed; yet nobody seemed, on the surface at least, to care. Gale Hanson at the dinner table had appeared to care more than most. But she might just be making something from nothing— which was almost possible to believe, until I had seen Curly Davis being stabbed.

Why had he been killed? The two men had been arguing violently; then Curly struck out at the other and he was killed immediately, without so much as a warning. King had been annoyed to distraction when I'd all but walked in on him and his foreign friend. Why?

The questions were too complex, the information too incomplete.

Finishing my cigarette, I decided to attempt to find Gale Hanson. Maybe she could tell me more about Judy's death. Then there was Val King. How much did she know about her father's real activities?

I hesitated over that last question, realizing that there was no doubt in my mind about the Castle of Eros not being what it appeared. Andrew King was involved in something quite illegal—beyond the establishment of the Cult, itself.

Turning, I looked at Sue, naked from the waist up, curled on the bed, like a little child. Yet she had sex appeal as a woman also. It was strange that we had not made love during the night. Yet this was the only woman I'd met, so far, whom I really desired in the way a man desires another *person,* a woman he truly likes. I liked Sue; I wanted to kiss and caress her, I desired very strongly to give pleasure to this dainty little Oriental. Yet nothing had happened during the night.

I slipped from the room, moved down the hall.

The house was quieter than the last time I'd been wandering through it. Apparently many people were sleeping it off.

Going downstairs, I became aware of voices in the main living room. Making my way there, I determined to start a serious investigation, questioning anybody I met -though indirectly, so there would be no suspicion as to what I was really up to.

The room was almost empty. A couple of strangers were in the corner. Rita Roselanda sat in the sofa next to a stocky man—a casual—just watching the roaring fire in the fireplace in front of them. Cherry Florence sat by herself at the bar, sipping a drink. Her bronze face flashed me an inviting smile as my eyes met hers. Immediately I moved toward her. She was a strikingly beautiful black woman, largely built, with wide shoulders, big-boned stature. She was wearing a cocktail dress that dipped very low between her breasts, revealing their full bulk, just hiding the nipples.

"Hello," she greeted, lifting her glass toward me. "You're the new guy, aren't you?"

"Yes, we met at dinner, last night." I slipped onto the bar stool next to her, fascinated by the stark beauty of her face and figure.

"How about a drink with me?" she suggested, lifting a bottle from behind the bar. "Gin...best drink there is. Just straight gin over the rocks. And an olive—if you wish."

"Forget the olive, Straight gin," I instructed. "It's quieted down some, hasn't it?"

"For a while. Everybody needs a rest...some are sleeping it off. But things will begin to pick up shortly. People will wander down one at a time or in pairs, in search for food, or drink. Some will swap with other couples and go outside or into bed-rooms—or merely find a cozy little place downstairs to enjoy themselves. The casuals are usually out for a weekend of kicks and can't get enough of what we have to offer."

"You sound rather bored with it all," I commented, sipping the drink that she had handed me, "Tastes good."

"I'm casual about everything—except a man. I strip for a living, you know." She gave me a toothy grin. "Like to see my act?"

The invitation was obvious. The idea sounded

appealing. Her big body was perfectly shaped, with well formed, firm-looking breasts. I could easily imagine that she would be able to give a very erotic strip show. With much pleasure following.

"I imagine there will be other chances to see you go through your routine."

"You don't like me?" She frowned.

"I think you are one of the most beautiful women I've ever seen. You certainly have a wonderful build."

"Against Blacks?"

"People are people. When I was in Vietnam I learned that, fast. Owe my life to Smitty, a young boy from Watts who was in the riots. It depends on what kind of person you are—regardless of color," I stated with some emotion.

"But you wouldn't want your sister marrying one?" she countered with a stiff smile.

For a moment I felt antagonism from her, then realized it was just a standard question. "I don't know quite how to answer that question with a simple yes and no. In the United States, most people are against it. For the children of such a marriage things can be difficult. In England that's something else. Someday there won't be any color line. People will be accepted for what they are as human beings, regardless of color."

Cherry Florence considered me with her large dark eyes, then asked: "Want to go to bed with me?"

I looked more carefully at Cherry Florence, trying to think of her as a sexual creature, exciting in body—which she obviously was—and felt a mixture of emotions. On the sexual side I could hardly hesitate at seeking physical pleasure with her body.

The flesh was smooth and silky and very dark. Her features were fine, delicate.

Suddenly the idea of climbing into bed with this big woman was startlingly exciting. I found myself almost immediately responding to the thought. There was a voluptuousness to the concept that far out-rated the actual act. At once I questioned my re-actions, wondering if it was because of her black skin that I felt excitement at merely thinking of sleeping with her; or was it because she was so beautiful? I realized that my own open-mindedness was not totally honest; there had developed within me a sub-conscious conditioning from childhood that made it impossible to react emotionally the same way my adult mind could logically work it out.

"You know," she said conversationally, refilling her glass, "this is the first time I've really talked to a white person so frankly. If only we could be given a good chance. I mean...sure there are lazy guys on my side of the fence. But damn it, you can't grow up emotionally healthy when your father, regardless of education, is still a laborer. You see young fellows going to school, studying hard—becoming A students and still not able to get good positions. We want what everybody else wants: an even break. If we make money, we should be able to spend it the same as anybody else. We should be able to go into the top hotels, join the same clubs, attend the same theaters, live in the same high-rent, high property tax sections of the city. But we can't even if we make money. That's what is so blasted irritating about it all."

She gulped down her gin, then gave me a flashing, hot look. "About that question...like to make love to me? We could go into the next room. I'll show you some tricks I learned in stripping. A stripper has the ability to do things that the ordinary woman can't do. Our body muscles are developed to move at will. I know tricks the guys really enjoy." She laughed throatily. "I taught Val all her tricks—but kept a few of my own. Val's a good dancer, and she uses her body good in sex with men—I've seen her work...but that's nothing compared to what I've learned. Want to try me out?"

I was suddenly burning all over with the idea. She placed a large hand on my thigh, squeezed. "I think we could have some fun."

For the first time I realized that Cherry was quite drunk. She stood, took my hand and led me to a door to the left of the bar. Once inside the room, she closed the door behind her.

Cherry did a slow grind of her hips, raised her arms high above her head, then with a quick movement of her right hand, unzipped the back of her dress. Then her body seemed to snake out of the gown, revealing the fact that there were only two pastie stars over her nipples and a flickering star at the very center of her womanhood. She bumped and ground her hips rapidly, flesh and muscles trembling. Her hands ran quickly over her body, caressing as every muscle tensed, quivered as if in orgiastic pleasure. She opened her mouth and a pointed tongue wetted its surface.

"You know," she said conversationally in that husky bedroom voice of hers, "the first white I had was a real card. He came back into my dressing room one night, lay down two hundred dollar bills, said 'Blackie, I like your act. Here's a tip for the finish, just you and me. Do it up good, Blackie and I'll give you another.' He was a pasty-faced, heavy type with a barrel chest. Immediately he stripped down to nothing and told me to do the same. I considered the offer. I'd never sold my body, but two bills just for letting a guy have me...well the temptation was pretty large. I'd never had a white before and the idea sounded appealing. So, since I'd been drinking a little, I shrugged. Decided to do it for him. He started grabbing my body in beefy, sweaty hands. He pawed my breasts, like this," her hand covered one breast, working it around and around, hard and violently. The pastie fell and she started pinching the nipple between two black fingers until it was hard and stiff. Her hips all the time were bumping and grinding.

"Then he touched me here," she announced, caressing the most intimate star she wore. "Then his hand clawed at my thigh, thus," and her hand clutched and clawed, seeming to bruise it. "I guess he went wild after that. I could see he was already ready to do it to me. So...it was very quick. I experienced such a voluptuous thrill over the whole thing—especially because he was a white guy. Later I did my best to find white lovers. I don't know...I thrill big to white flesh. They say guys of my own race are supposed to be bigger and better—and they can last a long time —but I go off easy, you see, and I like white meat."

Her body was now glistening and her breath came in heavy panting actions that bobbed her breasts up and down. Those large breasts seemed to be rolling, jerking, bouncing all on their own. She had wide hips and thick, but tapering thighs, muscular and strong. Her waist was narrow and stomach hard with a dancer's muscles. There was animal sexual excitement about her and what she was doing.

Suddenly Cherry bent backwards, going completely over, hands touching the floor. Then she swung slowly up, trembling, speaking all the time, "I like to do that kind of thing. Good for the woman's muscles." Standing upright she slowly began a split, trembling, every muscle quivering. She looked up at me, winked wickedly. "This is good for the thigh muscles. I can do things with my thighs that make men feel real good. Want me to show you?"

I stood there amazed by her routine, the casual manner in which she moved and talked at the same time.

Slowly coming upright again, Cherry said, "I did things to a guy with my thighs which sent him wild. He begged for more until there was...well there isn't a trick I don't know." Her hands covered those large breasts, then came away, pulling the other pastie star off. The nipples were large and brown, stiffly tight.

"How do you want it? Why don't you get dressed and—"

Just then the door opened and Kathy Sherman and a man stepped in.

The guy's face went chalk white as he saw Cherry Florence.

Kathy laughed. "Continue. Do the whole routine, so we can watch."

The man cursed. "A nigger. Dirty little nigger."

Cherry turned toward the man, her face contorting with sudden emotion. "What's with you, don't you like us Blackies? Wouldn't you like to put me on the floor and sex it up?"

She moved at him like a bull, pushing the man against the wall before he could do anything about it. Her hips drove against his, her breasts rubbed against the man's chest. "Come on, white man, get excited—show me how big a white ape you are. You white men can't do nothing good. Weak little body with limp hot dogs! A black boy is better, bigger and lasts longer. That's why you hate us. Isn't it? Come on, let's see if you know how to make a real woman excited. Come on, white man."

Her hands reached around and squeezed into his buttocks as her hips danced torturously against his. The man was obviously responding violently to her sexual provocation as any male animal would. Then all at once he fairly screamed, his face crazed with emotions. He shoved her away, fairly tore at his clothing.

I glanced at Kathy, who was panting, wide eyed with excitement. It was easy to guess she would get a real physical thrill by watching the show.

Cherry Florence glided, hips bumping and grinding all the way, to the round sofa-bed, lay down, stretching, all the time trembling in every muscle.

Her hands caressed away the last star on her body and began caressing her body in voluptuously long movements.

The white man suddenly dove at her, more bent at rape than anything else. She grabbed at his body and it was obvious from the beginning that Cherry

100

was in total command of the situation.

I turned, disgusted. "Come on, Kathy," I said, starting for the door, "Let's get out of here."

"Are you kidding?" she cried, staring at the two naked people. Her lips were half-parted and her face blanched in passion. A convulsive shudder came over her. "It's going to be great!" she rasped between quivering lips.

I fairly rushed out of the room, on the point of vomiting.

I half ran through the house, then outside, across the patio. Automatically, without realizing where I was going, I made my way toward the small beach. All I could think of was getting out of there, fast, breathing clean air. With an effort I controlled the urge to vomit. Finally, when my head cleared, I was standing on the beach, looking out across the ocean, breathing heavily.

Then as realization flooded back, I turned, searched the beach.

My first thought was how foolish it had been to come down here, I'd have to sneak away again, since it seemed dangerous to be the one who discovered Curly Davis' body.

I wasn't prepared to find Curly's body had disappeared.

MURDER MOST TERRIBLE! BY CHARLES NUETZEL

Chapter Eleven

I went directly to the place where the body of Curly Davis had fallen. There was no indication that any body had been there; no blood stains, nothing. I searched for some fifteen minutes, then was about to dig in the sand when the sound of footsteps came from the direction of the Castle of Eros.

Quickly I took a cigarette from my pocket lighted it, and sat down on the sand, pretending I was there just for some sun-tan.

Nervously I awaited the person or persons coming from the house.

As the footsteps came closer, I casually turned, to discover a barefoot young woman making her way in my direction. She was quite drunk.

Waving the cigarette, I greeted, "Hello."

"Hello, there," a light musical voice replied, "Nice day for a swim."

I thought she must be one of the casuals. I hadn't met her before.

"Say, you're the man Val picked after her dance," she exclaimed, sounding quite delighted. "Mind if I join you?"

I examined her figure with pleasure. She had high breasts, her hips were a little broad, but I like a woman shaped that way. I guessed her to be in her middle thirties. Her black hair was clipped fairly short. She wore a blouse half-opened in front, with no bra underneath. Her breasts pushed out against the cloth, and one nipple could be seen through the gap of an unbuttoned portion of the blouse.

She half fell to the sand and weaved back and forth, her eyes large, lips thick and pouty, struggling to shape a kiss. Then the woman's head seemed to jerk toward me, and I felt her lips cushion themselves against mine.

"Hello!" she managed to explode a moment later. An alcoholic thickness was evident in her speech as she added, "You're sho-kay."

I laughed, relieved to see that she was not quite able to take herself very seriously. Tossing her head, she said: "I'm Shirley...Shirley Peterson. My second time around. I take it you are new."

"New—but living in."

"Oh," a darkened eyebrow rose, impressively. "Then there will be many chances to learn all the secrets of what make you a man...later. That's the trouble with the casuals—it's now or never. Sorta fun, though. But with you regulars it's easy— if not now, next time." She laughed, patting my cheek with an awkward caress.

"You seem to know a lot about the place," I put in conversationally.

"Enough."

"How you learn about us?"

"Oh, through several contacts," she announced vaguely.

"Know King long?"

"Just as long as I've been on the island. Though

I did meet Val casually at a party—through Curly. Say, have you seen him, lately?"

I forced control over every facial muscle. "No. Not since after dinner. The two of us talked some before everybody arrived. Why?"

"Oh, we were supposed to meet sometime during the night—he promised me a roaring good time." Shirley gazed up into my eyes, as if having a hard time focusing. "Say, how about it? Maybe now is better than later. Curly isn't around and, as the boys say, any port in a storm."

"Mind if I take a rain-check on that, Shirley?" I asked, kissing her cheek to make it sound good.

"Rain-check, no. A passion-promise, yes. Actually, come to think of it, I'm a little tired out. Was left high and dry—or almost—by some foreign guy. Weren't no fun, that. I woke to find myself all alone." She shrugged. "You know, that's one thing I hate, being left, afterwards. My ex-husband used to do that. A girl likes to think she's desirable enough to be with after the storm is over. A little touch, a little affection to make her feel as if it was something more than just...bang-bang and over. Well...guess I better slip back to the party—maybe the action is swinging and I'm missing out on all the fun." She started to get up, but I restrained her.

"Wait. Can't you stay around a bit. I don't feel like being alone right now," I told her, attempting to sound pleading.

Her eyes burned bright as they seemed to strip down my body. "Taking that passion-promise up, now, after-all?"

"Just company; conversation." When I saw her reaction to that, I added: "And who knows what might happen after that?"

She relaxed, took hold of my hand and slipped it under the blouse, against one hot breast. *"Now* if you want to talk, do it with your hands as well as your mouth." She laughed coarsely at the line, then seemed to suddenly sober. "How the hell will I find Curly this way?"

"Why find him?" I countered. "Surely any port in a storm will do."

She grinned. "Only thing is, I...well, never mind."

There was something about her attitude which suddenly warned me that she might not be quite as drunk as she'd been attempting to appear. I don't know what clued me, but from then on I played it very carefully.

"What's this big flame between you and Curly?"

"Oh, he's been trying to put it to me for some time, now. We just never made the point. So. I promised myself that he had to do it...this time or else."

Her words were a little too bold, as if attempting to sound crude, yet not quite making it feel natural

"Kiss me," she offered, without warning. Her lips pouted under mine, her arms slipped about my neck. As that body drew itself up against me. I felt little resistance to her invitation, yet somehow I could not help believing it was an act played out for the sole purpose of distracting the conversation.

Her lips, warm and moist under mine, were trembling. Their softness sent a wave of desire through me. I found myself crushing her tightly in my arms. As we came up for breath, Shirley gasped out against my cheek, "Boy, you kiss!"

My right hand was just moving into her blouse, intent on bringing our little session to a more dramatic level of physical contact, when suddenly an amused cough sounded from behind me.

I jerked as if struck by a physical blow.

Standing over the two of us was Andy King, robes flowing about his body, beard trembling slightly in the wind. "Well, hello, you two. Don't let me stop you."

Shirley Peterson immediately withdrew from my embrace, seemed to straighten her blouse, and then patted the short black hair surrounding her head.

I stood, grinning wolfishly, "Actually we were just kissing good morning."

"I doubt that. But I'm sorry to have broken into your love-session. Curly sent me to find Miss Peterson. He's been looking for her for some time, now."

King gave me a look which said all too clearly that he wished to be alone with Shirley.

I glanced at the woman and realized this was her desire, too.

"Sorry, love," she grinned, blowing me a kiss. "See you later, okay? We can continue our little play then."

With a shrug of her shoulders, which bounced those breasts under the now fully buttoned blouse, Shirley turned her attention to Andy King. "Take me to your leader," she laughed. "I've been wanting to see him for some time, and he keeps giving me the slip."

I wondered for a moment if I should warn Shirley that Curly was dead. But something stopped me—a quick glance from her large, dark eyes, the set determination of her mouth. There was something going on which went far deeper than murder, and somehow I had the impression that Shirley Peterson was not what she seemed, and knew exactly what she was getting into. Had she seen the dead body, too? Or was she involved with the foreign man whose knife had killed Curly? But King had claimed to have seen Curly Buck Davis. The implications were too confusing to make any real sense.

As I moved ahead of the two, I determined to do my best to follow them; find out what was really going on.

The mass of questions beginning to probe their way through my conscious mind were dizzying.

What had Shirley really been doing on the beach? *If* she had been acting drunk, why?

And most important: *what was the real mystery behind the Castle of Eros?*

As I moved up the sloping pathway toward the house, I searched desperately to find a hiding place, but there was none. Once I'd reached the top of the cliff, I turned, pulled out a cigarette, moved into the bushy shadows near the house and waited for Andy King and Shirley Peterson to appear. My wait was long and cold. When they did not appear after ten minutes, I sighed, moved into the open, went to the edge of the cliff and looked down. The beach was empty.

Lighting the cigarette, I felt abruptly alone, frightened. Everybody in the castle was a stranger who might be something more than a mere sexual partner.

But two women, I was sure, were what they appeared to be: Sue Kong and Gale Hanson. Gale had

108

revealed every indication of investigating Judy's death. I immediately determined to find her. With that in mind, I returned to the house, intent upon my search.

MURDER MOST TERRIBLE! BY CHARLES NUETZEL

Chapter Twelve

Trying to find one person in a large house without being found by others is hard enough, but in the case of Gale Hanson and the Castle of Eros, it seemed impossible during the first hours of the morning. I attempted to learn if others knew where she was, and in a couple of cases almost ended up having to go to bed with some woman who was rather insulted that I wasn't interested. The last thing I wanted to do was make passes at strange women. I bumped into Mic, who was arm-in-arm with some strange man—a casual. She blew me a kiss and said, "See you later," in such a way that it promised much.

"Where's Gale?" I asked.

"Haven't seen her all morning."

Finally I gave up and went to Sue Kong's room, knocked on the door and, when she answered, stepped in, closing the door after me.

"What's happened?" she inquired in a small, frightened voice. She sat up in bed, her breasts naked above the covers, eyes large, still frightened.

After I had told her about Andy King and Shirley Peterson—and the fact that Curly had disappeared from the beach—she seemed even more frightened than before.

"Oh, Bill," she half sobbed, leaning close, tiny hands clutching mine. "What can we do?"

"What's there to *do?* Nose around. I've been trying to find Gale—but no luck."

Sue nodded. "I was frightened when I awoke and found you missing."

"I'm sorry," was the only thing that came to mind to tell her. "There are a lot of things which need explaining. Isn't there anything more you can tell me?"

"I don't know..." She thought for a moment, then shrugged. "Maybe both of us should circulate and see what information we can get." Sue looked up at me, eyes frowning. "But...can't we...I wish I could get off this island. I'm scared, Bill. Really frightened."

"Why?"

"You saw what happened to Curly."

"But it happened for a reason—what that reason is we don't know but—"

"That's what scares me."

"Shouldn't. After all—Curly apparently did something, discovered something, said something—or *was* something...that created danger for him."

"What was Judy, then?"

"You connect the two?"

"They were both killed. There *must* be some connection. But what?"

"You said that during the special parties with the foreign guests it was necessary to keep to the house—ever wonder why?"

She nodded, tight-lipped. "All morning I've been wondering why. Something had to be going on *outside* which they didn't want us to know about. But what?"

"I've come to the same conclusions. Andrew King is involved in some illegal activity with a foreign nation and Judy discovered by accident what that was. So did Curly—and that guy you said you met..." I suggested, hammering away at my points with almost angry intent. "The danger lies in discovering facts you have no business knowing, and then being found out."

"Bill, let's get out of here," Sue pleaded, throwing her arms about my neck. Her soft cheek pressed longingly against mine. I was aware of the stiff points of her breasts biting my chest. How lovely and desirable she was. I felt the heat of passion lace its way through my body, bubbling up through the blood streams, waving across one nerve passage after another.

I became aware of the fact that this was the only girl I'd met in the last couple of days whom I really desired, with whom I wanted to share the beauty of love, of giving—yet had not made any real headway.

That was strangely perverse.

Sue threw back her head, wide lips parted, and then kissed mine. "Please," she murmured, "Get me off the island. I'm scared to death."

"How?"

"The boat."

"Do you know how to operate one?" I inquired.

"No—but it surely isn't that hard. *Please,* Bill." Her grasp tightened about my neck.

"We can't just leave—without learning the truth," I countered helplessly, feeling the blood throbbing at my temples. The soft nearness of her dainty body was slowly driving me to a great peak of desire that would not be controllable for much longer. Either I got out of there, or we would be making love. Strangely enough, though it was the right place for such things, it was the wrong time. Our timing seemed totally off because of circumstances involving the murder of Curly Buck Davis. I could almost hate the man.

"Sue," I managed to say, gently pushing her away, "There are things I have to do—for private reasons—can you believe that?"

She nodded, tight-lipped, as if she were about to cry. I pulled her gently close, my arm around her. "You're the first girl I've met for a long time that I cared about. I don't know why—but it is probably because of what we both witnessed. Sue—in the right time I want to make love to you—not just a *sex* party. You understand?"

She smiled up sweetly at me. "I guess I understand. Something more important than just a party. That's nice, really, Bill. I've almost forgotten what *it's* like that way. But why me?"

"Why anybody? The thing is, this isn't the time to start playing anything more serious than sexual games—I just can't stomach the idea with you— doing it like that...cheap and—"

Tears were suddenly streaming down Sue's high cheeks. "Why me? You *know* *what...I've*...become...cheap and dirty. I've dishonored my father and..."

I cupped her delicate face between my hands.

"Sue, don't be silly. We're adults. We're single. We're normal human beings. Everybody does some-

114

thing like this—either going out to bars and dating anything that attracts us, or more honestly—like this. Which one is less moral...I really can't tell you. Our cultural attitudes are changing—our thoughts about sex have changed. Not too long ago women weren't supposed to like sex—and probably had every reason not to like it too much, because the men didn't make any real effort to make it interesting to them. Hell, women have liked sex as long as men have attempted to make it pleasurable for them. So, don't start acting silly."

Her short sobs came to an end. Looking up at me, she smiled. "Silly, really. It just touched me. It's the first time any guy said he cared even that much. I know you aren't talking about love...but rather a romantic affair—that's different than what we have here. Maybe...maybe that's really what I've been looking for—but didn't know how to go about getting it." She shrugged. "We're making fools of ourselves. But...I guess that's necessary, too."

The last riddle made little sense to me, but I said: "Look, Sue. The only thing between a man and woman is sexual attraction, companionship and finally romantic love. The games played out here are nothing but sexual exercises, a means to learn something about yourself and grow that much more. Its not how a person grows and matures, but that they do, in time, realize the right balance. Some people never do. I think this experience has changed my attitude some. What counts between two people is what they feel for each other—respect is only a point of view. Sexual love should be a logical outgrowth of desire and companionship. It develops by naturally experiencing the most intimate and beautiful relationship between man and woman, maturely, out of affection, tenderness and the desire to give pleasure, not just take it." I pulled her into my arms, gently kissed her lips. "I want to be tender to you, Sue. I want it to be right."

She nodded as I released her. "So, you want to nose around a little?"

"I have to find something out, Sue. Believe me, it's important." I nodded as if in thought. "If you can—maybe it might be a good idea to join me—we can split and then compare notes. But for heavens sake, don't even hint what you have learned and—"

"You know what they say about the Oriental? Ah, so, Ah, so." She bowed, a frozen smile on her face. "Little Lotus Flower will smile, be nice little girl and while evil man is sleeping will slip knife between his ribs."

Her take-off was startling, for it brought back memories of the Second World War, when I was just old enough to sense that fear of the Japanese, the horror of the Germans. How time and history can change a person's viewpoint. And maturity. The whole western civilization had changed a lot since the Second World War; especially the American public. In the forties, war had been played out as some kind of game—not as happily as some twenty years before—and then Korea, in the fifties, removed the glamour from war, and finally the Viet Nam conflict crushed all belief that war was a glory road. War was hell. People were people. There were good people and there were bad ones, in every country.

How I wanted to make love to Sue Kong, but instead I stood, said: "Just be careful. We'll meet

116

here..."

"Sometime after four. Okay?" she suggested, slipping out of bed, unashamedly exposing her totally naked body to my sight.

The desire swelled to a great pain, both physical and emotional. I wanted to ravish her and at the same time caress, touch, kiss, love, be tender, to smell the roses along the way through the heavenly paths to her ecstasy. I wanted to have it with everything beautiful surrounding us. I wanted to slip my arms about her delicate form and tenderly surrender to the loveliness of what was in her soul. Our bodies would follow our spiritual union long after we'd become one in mind. And only then would we actually mate in some fury of passion. I wanted her in a way a man what's a woman he truly cares about; a woman he could love. Surely all that as illusion; but what a beautiful one. And that was stunning!

Sighing, I moved to the door. "Just be careful, Sue."

She smiled blankly at me, winked, and then clawed out at the air like a cat. "You'd be surprised how careful little Sue can be."

But there was a light edge of fear still hidden in her eyes. Strangely, this little girl was helping me, not even knowing the full reasons. I realized that it would not be hard to really fall in love with Sue; regardless of what she had been. After all, how does a guy really know what his girl was like before he met her? All of life is an act we play out for the sake of others. Someone like Sue Kong could easily fool a fellow into thinking she had never slept with anybody. She looked innocent; so much the child. Yet her experience was obvious.

My nerves throbbed with excitement at the very thought of holding that dear form in my arms again, at the proper time and place.

Chapter Thirteen

The next hour was fruitless. I wondered through the Castle, from room to room. Several times I walked into a love-session, once between two girls. One was stripped down to her waist, the other had total attention centered upon kissing large pointed nipples. Fascinated, yet wanting to turn away and immediately walk out, I found myself watching the two lesbian lovers. It was some time before I realized that the girl doing the seducing was none other than Val King. She kissed those large breasts as if she couldn't get enough of the feasting. Then her hands started working on the other girl's skirt, pulling it down, half tearing the cloth. "Watch out!" the other complained. "Take it easy." Val fairly snarled, "Shut up!" and continued pulling on the skirt until it had fallen at the other's feet. Then Val's hands worked on the black garter belt, then shaking fingers caressed the nylons down over beefy thighs and legs. Finally Val tore off the last piece of cloth that had covered her main target. Before attacking, Val feasted her eyes upon her intended victim, trembling with passion.

It was then that I turned and got out of there fast. Neither woman had been aware of my presence.

I bumped into Rita Roselanda, jarring into those large bouncy soft breasts. She laughed and tightly embraced me, her hips flush against mine. "Let's make the scene," she suggested huskily. One look in the woman's eyes and I realized she was close to being smashed to the brain tubes.

"Sorry, no time," I countered, reluctantly kissing her lips. That hungry tongue of hers lanced out, almost choking me.

A moment later I was moving away from Rita, a hot reaction flushing through my body at that quick, intimate contact.

Several couples moved in and out of the hallway, some half naked. A young girl with nice looking breasts and a rounded body stepped from a doorway, took one look at me, and grinned, "Where've you been keepin' yourself, big boy?"

I avoided willing arms, smiling at her pert breasts.

Making my way to the main lounge for a drink, I decided that it might be better if I played along with the next girl at least for a short sexual session—for appearance's sake. Luckily I met no resistance all the way to the small home bar. There I stood next to a young man sitting, pale-faced, against the bar, a drink in his hand.

"What's wrong?" I asked conversationally, pouring myself a stiff scotch, straight.

"Nothing," he answered, turning to look at me. His soft, large eyes seemed to caress my body. A slow smile formed on his lips. "Say, what do you think of these bitches?"

"Don't know what you mean."

120

"Whores, all of them. Cheap little sluts. I never could understand such women. None of them like they made Mother."

I laughed nervously. "We don't know what Mother really was like, do we?"

He shrugged, reached out, and touched my shoulder. "You are terribly good-looking."

"If you're making a pass, forget it," I cautioned. "I like girls, only."

"What's with you? This is the world of Eros. All things go."

"Each picking their own form of pleasure, friend," I shot back, feeling an icy hand of cold nausea eat at me.

"I like boys best, but I'll swing with the bitches. Long as they know how to kiss right—and where to kiss." He gave a high-pitched laugh. "A girl has to do it just like a guy."

Disgusted, I walked away, moved across the room, trying hard to understand why homosexual acts between men seemed more wrong than lesbian acts between women. Shrugging off the thought, I settled down in a corner of the room, away from most of the activity. There were about five other people in the room besides the gay one and myself:

Three women and two men.

Two of the women were having conversation, both verbal and physical, with one of the men. It was interesting in a perverse sort of way to watch how the guy moved and the women responded. His right hand was keeping itself occupied with one woman's breasts, the other hand explored a nicely exposed thigh, where he had worked the other girl's skirt upwards. The two women seemed delighted by

121

their companion. For some moments I didn't realize that the one with her skirt pulled up was Gale Hanson. Only when she happened to meet my gaze did I recognize her.

"Gale," I called. "Where have you been keeping yourself?"

She laughed, then said something to the guy who immediately removed his hand from her. Standing, Gale rearranged her skirt and glided across the room toward me. "Hello, Bill, I was wondering about you, too."

The woman was half drunk, her eyes glazed with what could be nothing other than sexual excitement and drink.

She immediately moved close and then slipped onto my lap, sliding her arms about my neck. "Ever since last night at the dinner table, I hoped we would meet. How about us sharing?"

"I thought you were occupied with your friend over there."

"Oh, *him?* We were just playing around. He did a few tricks with me this morning. I was considering exploring more possibilities with him in a short time, but would much rather say, 'Sorry 'bout that,' and try something with you." She pressed her wide mouth against mine.

There was something starkly sensual about Gale, even though she was hardly what one would call a beauty. Yet her eager directness was exciting. I placed a hand on her thigh, high up, pressing into the soft flesh. She kissed my mouth, her tongue running along my lips. "Let's go some place," she suddenly suggested, tensing against me. "I'd rather be intimately alone with you."

122

"Why not?" If only she knew the real reason for my wanting to get her alone.

We stood and I finished off my scotch. "I want to get another drink, first."

"I have a bottle in my room, Bill," she said eagerly, "Come on. Let's get going. I'm only hot."

I found it hard to keep from laughing at Gale. There was something comic about her. Watching her face, I noticed she must be just about my own age, in her early thirties. An eager little secretary out to get thrills which probably had never come to her before Eros.

We moved across the room, her hip bumping mine with every step. She took my right hand, which had been holding her slender shoulder, and slipped it under her arm, pressing the fingers against her breasts.

Whispering in my ear, she said: "I'm so burning I could do it right here and now."

"Not me, Gale," I assured her.

Suddenly Gale stopped and twisted around; her body whipped against mine. The softness of her was highly thrilling. The movement of her hips as they jerked back and forth surged a sudden lust into me that could easily have made it quite possible to connect with her right there in front of all the others.

Laughing throatily, she said: "That felt good, I can't wait until we can do it naked."

My own passions had hit a new high. Suddenly I didn't really care whose body I found my relief with. The liquor had started to do its work.

We almost raced down the hall, into the lobby, up the steps. We found an empty room and slammed the door behind us. Gale locked it.

"This your room?" I inquired.

"No, but I can't wait," she moaned, pulling off her black sweater and then slipping out of the skirt in quick, nervous movements. "Hurry, undress."

I felt her expectation and excitement reach out across the room towards me, softly choking, building the need to a hard driving force. My own hands began to pull at the clothing that confined my body.

Gale, quicker at getting undressed, because she wore no bra, came at me like a charging bull. Her hands grabbed at my belt buckle and ripped the pants down. Caressing hands did the rest of the work of making me naked. She was so eager that all I could do was stand there, amazed, unable to move. Then what happened was almost as startling, for Gale couldn't wait any longer. She moved, and her lips were all over me at once, then I felt the pressure of that almost awkward body against mine. She pushed me toward the bed, hands caressing me in such a way that my eyes shut against the pleasure of it. Suddenly I fell backwards on the bed and Gale was on top of me, continuing her caressing, her lips now running all over me, as if she couldn't control herself.

"Oh, Bill, this is going to be good, so good, I can tell it. Oh, boy, I like you...like all of you."

Her hands now went to work on me with such intent and purpose that all I could do was lie there and enjoy it. Then all at once she moved and I felt soft flesh against mine. I realized that my legs were hanging over the edge of the bed and Gale was almost standing over me, hips working frantically. The pleasure was fantastic. But as it mounted, building, I knew it wouldn't be long before it was impossible to control myself. Then, just as I was about to grab at her, Gale's thighs held me in a soft warm embrace and a wave of physical joy waved through every nerve.

Gale gasped, laughed, moaned, then moved downwards and as her body positioned itself for the final plunge, I felt soft lips cover mine and the thrust of a tongue slashed deep into my mouth in total rhythm with the sudden downward movement of her hips that joined our bodies in complete physical union.

From this very beginning, Gale controlled everything like some demon lover. Her hips made the movements, slowly and smoothly, torturing me with pleasure. But when the action built in rhythm I knew this would not last long. Neither of us was in the mood to wait, unable to sustain the joy longer. I grabbed her body, crushing it downwards as the explosion of rockets totally drove me off the bed.

The two of us strained like metal about to snap in two, shuddered, convulsively locked together, and then fell on the bed, exhausted, spent out, savoring the aftermath of our sexual union.

Black clouds folded about my mind and time seemed to stand still.

It was some time after my little session with Gale Hanson that consciousness returned. Gale was sitting up in bed, looking down at me, and smoking a cigarette. Her deep-set eyes seemed to be darkly hidden, their expression hard to understand. It was as if she were studying some strange kind of bug, an alien creature.

"You slept for some time, lover," Gale announced a little coldly. Her attitude was detached, distant. "I was wondering when you would come out of it."

"How long?"

"Oh...about twenty minutes."

I smiled, then a short laugh broke from me. "Twenty minutes after what you did? What do you expect?"

"I don't know." She seemed sober, slightly retreated within herself. "I just don't expect to sit, smoking, and—most of all—thinking."

Chapter Fourteen

"What about?"

"None of your business, really."

"What's wrong?"

"What could be wrong? We made sex and now we will make sex again—either now or later. It's really as simple as that, isn't it? That's the whole idea of Eros; finding a partner, sharing and sharing again, no thoughts of love, no thoughts of emotions getting in the way—just sex for sex's sake and the total physical sharing."

"You don't sound very happy about it."

"Don't be silly," Gale laughed sharply. "I'm happy about it. People need sex. It's like a food. Once you learn to accept your body as a hungry thing, and then once you learn how to find a means of satisfying all its hungers—without getting hurt, what's the difference?"

"What about the emotional hunger?" I countered, reaching for her cigarette, which she readily released for me.

"Emotions are things that children play with—"

"And adults learn to experience maturely, don't you think?" After taking a drag of the cigarette I handed it back to her.

"Who wants emotional experiences? They are tricks one plays with one's self. Once you learn to accept yourself *in total,* you don't need anybody but yourself to live with."

"You'd be in bad shape without partners to..."

"Sex it up with?" She shrugged. "So...you socialize in a group like this one. You'd be surprised how many sex cults there are in the States. Oh, not like this one, to be sure. But what about the wife-swapping, the single people who run around, switching partners? It's all the same, really. Most clubs are sex clubs in one way or another. Conventions are sex clubs in a way. It's all the same. This one is different because it is just a little more honest about it. We come here to sex it up. We don't make any bones about it. We have a good life—live well...and don't have to think about life outside as long as we are here. People outside go about hurting each other simply to satisfy their personal egos. The boss goes about bossing—and that makes him or her feel good. *Big!* Reason: nine times out of ten it is either guilt feelings about sex or a bad sex life."

"Maybe you have something there." I searched the room. "Think there's anything to drink in here?"

For the first time a friendlier laugh came from Gale. "You know, maybe I *do* like you a little. Let's look."

The two of us slipped from the bed, and it was Gale who found a bottle of whiskey, half-filled. She opened it, took several swallows, handed the bottle over to me, and then went back to the bed.

After a couple of shots of whiskey I felt a little better and turned to face Gale, trying hard to understand her. She was an odd one, for sure. Different

128

than I'd expected.

"The bottle, please," Gale requested as I sat next to her on the bed. After another few swallows, she handed me the whiskey bottle, which I placed on the floor. For a moment she frowned. Then her wide, thin lipped mouth moved, said: "You seem different from the other guys here. Don't ask me why, I don't know...something...I just can't put my finger on it. I don't feel quite as...angry…no, that's not the word...well, never mind."

"It is all new to me. Like I said the other day— last night, only...so it was...so much has happened.... Came out of the service, heard about Judy from a friend of mine and—"

"Oh, yes, you were talking about Judy, weren't you?"

"Not really, just listening. It was...come to think of it, I don't know who started up the conversation."

She smiled gently, reached out, and touched my cheek. "I don't know either...but—I felt as if you wanted to talk about her more."

"Something like that. It was a shock." I picked up the bottle, offered it to Gale.

"It was a shock to most of us, too. But several strange things have happened here, you know." She took another swallow from the whiskey bottle.

"Like?"

"The special parties...a lot of foreigners—have to stay in the house...I don't know." She shrugged again, and it was beginning to be obvious that the whiskey was gaining its effects over her body.

"What do you know about Judy's death?"

"What makes...you say that?"

She leaned closer, placed a possessive hand on

my leg.

"You said it, last night. Don't you remember?" Her face frowned in thought.

"Not really."

On a hunch, I reached for the bottle, took several mock swallows, and then handed it to Gale, who greedily had herself a stiff jolt.

"You're a fine woman, Gale," I announced grandly, again playing a sudden hunch. Some of the things she had said so far indicated that she was highly unhappy. Her attitude towards me suggested guilt about this life she led here on Eros.

Her mouth widened in a large grin. The hand on my leg moved upwards to the thigh, squeezed. "I like you, too."

"I mean it, Gale. Last night I realized you were different from the rest. I don't know...I think you care a little more than you let on."

She beamed at me. Her fingers squeezed my thigh again.

"And you surely know...how to make love." I reached out, caressed her breasts lightly. "You feel nice. I like your breasts."

"Why don't...you kiss them?" She giggled, thrust out her chest.

I played lightly with their nipples until they were hard points between my fingers. She half closed her eyes, moaned slightly, a sweet smile on her mouth.

"Let's have another drink," I suggested when her right hand moved more intimately close to my hips. It was obvious that another session was in the offing, and at the moment I wanted to question her.

After another couple of swallows of whiskey,

she leaned closer, circled my neck with slender arms.

"You were saying, Gale...about Judy."

"Judy? Judy? Oh, Judy. But we weren't talking about Judy." She kissed my lips.

Gently I urged her away. "A little bit. Give a guy some rest, honey. I want to do it right with you; for you. You're so great you just wore me out." I forced a laugh.

She frowned at me for a moment then laughed, too. "Okay...'bout Judy."

"Think...what is it you know about her?"

"She was a bitch...in heat." Her words then began to come out a little more controlled. It was as if the booze was now affecting her to the point where, if she centered all her attention on talking, it was possible to appear quite sober. "But...she was a nice girl. It was horrible—I discovered her body...before the others...I didn't tell anybody about that." Abruptly Gale stiffened, stared at me, and then seemed to be frightened. "I never told anybody about *that!* Why you?"

"Gale, come on, don't be foolish." I caressed her breasts, then palmed one in my hand, tenderly squeezing.

"That feels so good."

Her eyes closed, mouth hung half-open and there was nothing I could do but accent the pleasure of the caress by kissing her lips. After the tongue-dancing kiss, I said: "What did you discover?"

"I saw...it happen...King was there...or at least I think...he was, somebody like him, and another man. No, it couldn't have been King he was dressed in a business suit. But looked like...Andy." Gale frowned again, her features pinching together. "Also...a small, dark-haired girl...dressed in a bathing suit and.... Oh, kiss me, please kiss me all over...."

"Gale...it's important. What did you see?" I shook her violently by the shoulders.

She stared up at me as if slapped. "What do you want to know?"

"About Andy King. And the others. Who was the girl?"

She stared at me for a moment, shook her head. "I didn't see anything...not what you are saying, anyway. I just saw them...on the path up from the beach...I...was sure they must have..." Her eyes looked down at me and a greedy expression burned there. With her right hand she reached out and the caress which touched me sent a wild erotic pleasure through my body.

"Who was the girl?"

"Sue...Sue Kong," she said, all attention on what she was doing.

Suddenly Gale shoved me backwards against the bed with such force that I was stunned. Then her head lowered over my hips.

The statement she had made now shot warnings through me like a knife. All I could think of was the immediate danger I was in. If Sue Kong and Andy King were in something together, and what had happened to Curly Buck Davis had anything to do with it, I was marked for immediate death! But how could Sue be involved? It didn't make sense.

Suddenly what Gale wanted to do was being done and all attention knifed at her love actions. She was that erotic, that skilled, that demanding and passionate.

After that, my full attention was on Gale Hanson and her hungry love-making.

MURDER MOST TERRIBLE! BY CHARLES NUETZEL

134

Chapter Fifteen

The first thing I could think of, after Gale had finished with me, was getting away from Eros before it was too late.

For the first time in my life I almost felt like a male prostitute. And in a way, that was exactly what I'd become in the last two days. In order to get information, it was necessary to allow women to have their pleasure with me. Hardly an undesirable fate; but a depressing one for a man who believes in being the seducer rather than the seduced—regardless of the fact that a woman is always the seducer. What man can have a lady without her consent? Without raping her? A woman might, as the social game requires, seem to run from the man—but never fast enough not to be caught.

Thankfully, Gale was totally unconscious by the time my own wits returned. Gathering my clothing, I dressed, glanced at the woman and thought about how beauty is merely a thing of the mind. During the act of sexual intercourse one can imagine anybody—any shape. A breast, a nipple, a thigh, flesh, lips—the total woman is much the same, no matter what shape the body or color the hair. Understanding of this brought home another point: nor does the color of skin really matter that much. Only the personality; the motive; the reason for the union.

I was just about to slip out of the room when a thought startled me to inaction. My hand on the doorknob, I hesitated.

How much could I believe? What *could* I believe? Sue Kong had seemed honestly frightened; she had hidden away with me, had not turned me in to King. What kind of game would she be playing? And this Gale Hanson—what kind of game was she playing? Sue had seemed to really want to get off the island. Why hadn't Gale, knowing what she had told me? Was it that life on the continent, in the United States, was so terrifying for this plain secretary that she would rather live here, experiencing all sorts of sexual pleasure, than to return to another kind of hell? And if Sue Kong was actually working for King, and if King was involved with something really illegal, then why should she want to run away?

I checked my watch and realized that it was time to meet Sue.

Considering the thought that I had no way of getting off the island without help, there seemed nothing to do but keep my planned meeting with Sue.

Stepping out of the room, I made my way to where I'd last left Sue Kong. When I opened the door, I heard movement from the room beyond. There was very little light to meet me, but a soft voice said: "Bill...over here, the bed."

I moved through the darkness, a sinking feeling beginning to rush over me. What if she was naked? It seemed totally impossible to even consider making love again. A man's body will give just so much—and then it drops...not quite dead, but near to it. The session with Gale had exhausted all ability to even consider a woman desirable.

"Sue?" I groped through the darkness to the bed, and then came into contact with naked flesh.

Sue came into my arms, soft and warm, lovingly. She cradled her head against my still naked chest. For the first time in hours I remembered that I'd been walking about half naked even since the Dance of Passion the night before. How strange it is that a person can get so used to such a condition of undress. It made me consider the fact that all moral customs are only moral in the right circumstances. It even seemed possible, at that moment, to make love in front of a thousand faces, if that were the custom.

"Where have you been?" she half cried, small hands cupping my cheeks. "I've been worried."

"With Gale," I admitted honestly enough.

"What did you find out?"

"Enough."

"What?" she insisted.

In order to quiet her, more than anything else, I pulled that delicate body closer and found her lips in the darkness below mine. The kiss was so sweet and natural, so wonderful, that for a moment I forgot my questions about her. She tightened against me, totally nude.

"Oh, Bill, I've never felt this way about a man before. Oh, love me, dear Bill." She half dragged me to the bed, settled down upon it and urged me to her side.

The body can do many strange and wonderful things; maybe because the mind controls all. Maybe the condition of a man—or the lack of women over a long period of time—has a lot to do with it. Who knows?

The way Sue seemed to gently tangle her body around mine, legs trapping my legs, arms holding me close, lips cushioned softly to my mouth, created a truly powerful effect over me.

I held her—simply held her dear form close. There was a gentle submissiveness to the way Sue clung, like a little girl, a child fully trusting the lover. There was no urging, other than her nearness; no push, other than that which built slowly, so slowly, up through me. It was more a desire for tenderness, a need to give pleasure, that coursed itself through every nerve until I felt the first stir of desire for something more than closeness. I wanted to caress her, I wanted to know all the curves and hollows, the lovely softness of silken flesh. My lips covered Sue's and she responded tenderly, just a little movement, an attempt to bring herself nearer, though this was quite impossible. Our bodies were already stretched out tightly together, clinging flesh-to-flesh as one.

It seemed that one caress led to another, but for the first time since reaching Eros, I was the seducer; I was the one who aggressed upon the woman. My hands found the hollows, the full swell of breasts. My lips circled down across the pathway the caresses had followed, delighting in this total game of seduction. The time involved in making love to Sue might have been minutes, hours, or years, for time seemed to stand still. There were only the two of us in the darkness of the room. Orientation had disappeared. I wasn't on Eros, but in the private world of two lovers seeking each other, discovering the secrets of each other's body. As little trembles, little quivers, slight convulsions began to shake through Sue, her hands, like searching fingers of love, came out of the darkness to direct me, to pull me down further along the curves of her form to find the most sensitive areas, then finally they began their own search over me, like magic, sending sparks of pleasure and need, rebuilding the power and strength that had been lacking only a short time before.

This was the kind of love game I had craved all these months, these years, while away from the states in the filth and dirt of army life, which takes into account nothing but the fact that you are a body which can be directed to kill or be killed. This was the love of emotions. I thought of all the other women I had possessed, before, during and after the army, and none had given more joy than this moment. The thought flitted across my mind for but an instant as our bodies finally surged gently together, becoming one unit, both in flesh and that other substance one might call soul—for lack of a better name.

That first instant when we became one, I knew that for me, at least, the women of Eros, the life here, could never stand out as important other than to point out the contrast between sex games and love games. For sure, I was playing out the most fantastic love-game in the world, convincing myself that Sue Kong was a woman I loved, though I knew little about her, nor could I possibly really care about her as a true lover might. It was an infusion, but the kind upon which true love can develop and become a reality. Then the moment for such thoughts passed.

Our bodies, trained in the lover's game, moved, surged with the rhythm of love and finally the pure physical need, the lust of overwhelming passions took over and it was not much different from any other such act, except that the inner need to give pleasure rather than merely take it was strong.

Sue strained up against me, her arms embracing my form as a low, gasping sigh uttered from between tortured lips. I felt the erotic explosion unite me with Sue in this instant of total pleasure.

When we sank onto the bed, our forms now isolated from one another, I felt a surge of uncertainty. Gale Hanson's words about Sue Kong being with King—knowing about Judy's death, as a participant, sank in.

If Gale had been telling the truth, my life was now in danger—I'd been foolish to come back to Sue, foolish to have made love to her.

Sue sat up and I felt her leave the bed, heard her footsteps recede and then return. She sat down next to me.

As I opened my eyes, I saw Sue lighting a cigarette. She placed it between my lips and then lighted another.

For a long time neither of us spoke, but my own thoughts were churning, attempting to boldly state what Gale had told me, and to see how Sue took it.

Instead, when I did speak, my words were totally different than I'd expected them to be.

"What do you know about Judy's death?" I inquired.

She gave me a sharp look, blew smoke in the air, said: "What's that question mean?"

140

"Then...about Gale Hanson. What do you know about her?"

"Nothing much, really. What'd you learn?" Sue was accusing as she looked down at me.

"Just answer the questions, Sue. Please. I'll tell you everything...shortly." I sat up, looked intensely into her eyes.

"Only that she was a friend of Val and her father. They apparently knew each other before." Sue's eyes narrowed slightly. "What's so important about Gale?"

"She says you...well knew a lot more about Judy's death than you claimed."

Sue didn't say anything, for a moment. Then she asked: "Exactly what *did* she say?"

"That you were with King—that both of you were there on the beach with Judy and that she saw it all."

Sue nodded. "I was with King. She saw that? And what else did she say?"

"That King was in a business suit."

"And what else?" Her voice was strangely cold, the eyes continuing to narrow.

"That...well, she didn't say it was *you* for sure, nor did she say it was King for *sure,* but she did claim that it looked like both of you and—"

"How did you happen to find all this out?"

"I got Gale drunk."

"Drunk?" Sue was thoughtful for a moment. "How drunk, Bill. It's important."

"Very drunk, I'd say. She had a hard time speaking. She slurred. I gave her quite a lot of whiskey."

Sue stubbed out her cigarette, leveled her dark

eyes on me. "Gale never gets drunk. I've seen her pass out, but I've never seen her drunk. She can drink more than anybody I've ever known. She can drink until it comes out her ears—but drunk? No. Not the conventional way. She drinks and drinks—but never shows it other than getting tired. She'll just go off to bed. I don't know what it is...but she *never* gets drunk. Like some people can have one sip of liquor and be drunk, Gale can drink it up all night and never show any visual effects."

"You're kidding. That's impossible."

"Nothing's impossible—even Gale being drunk isn't impossible. But I'm telling you, Bill, it is not *very* possible. Something's going on...and what's your real interest in Judy? Don't lie. I've known there was an intense interest from the very beginning. Her lover? Is that it? Or...what?"

Sue's businesslike manner was startling. She didn't even seem the same woman.

"I don't know what you're talking about, Sue," I lied.

She grabbed hold of my arms, squeezing hard. Her face contorted with emotion. "Tell me the truth! It's important."

Without realizing what I was saying, my lips moved, spoke. "I'm her brother."

Sue's hands released me, lowered to her side. "That explains a lot."

"What are you talking about?"

"I was never with King on the beach. They know about us. I'm sure of it. Somehow they know what we saw on the beach this evening."

"But we can't prove anything." I countered, alarmed by her suggestion, because it now threw out

142

all of my first theories. "What will they do?"

"I don't know, Bill, but I think we better get out of here as fast as possible—after that..." She looked up pleadingly. "I want to get out of here. I'm no heroine, I'd rather live with what I know—and keep quiet—and *live!*"

"I guess there's nothing to running one of those boats. We could try," I suggested, standing and then hesitating. I had come to find out what had happened to my sister; running now would not get that accomplished.

"I have to stay," I told her.

"But why?"

"I have to find out who was responsible for Judy's death."

"Don't you know?" Sue inquired, as if it were quite obvious.

"No."

"Then think back a little. Regardless of what I tell you—which could obviously be a lie if you believe Gale Hanson's story. She was killed on the beach. We saw Curly killed by a foreigner. His body disappeared. Gale claims that King killed your sister—or that she saw him there—with me. Unless I'm crazy, I think Gale is involved with King, and now she knows you are involved with Judy in some way. They aren't dumb. They'll put two and two together and get the right answer. I'm scared. I want out of here as fast as possible."

I considered the facts. If she were telling the truth we were in danger by staying on the island. If she were not telling the truth, I was finished in either case.

"Okay. We'll split."

At that moment the door opened and three forms burst in: Gale Hanson, Andy King and the foreign man I'd seen—who had killed Curly on the beach. They quickly closed the door behind them.

King said, "Don't say a word, either of you."

The foreign man was holding an ugly looking .38, pointed in our direction.

King glanced at Gale, said, "You did the right thing. The only thing I'm sorry about is that Sue will suffer, too."

Gale laughed bitingly. "The little slant-eyed tramp doesn't deserve anything better."

"You will come with us" King commanded. "And you will not make any sound or action if we meet somebody along the way. It won't get you anywhere and only cause other innocent people to die. Do you understand?"

I merely nodded and Sue squeezed my hand, trembling, then nodded, too.

"I guess it would be foolish to ask what you have planned for us," I stated, starting slowly forward at King's command.

"Quite foolish, young man. But I don't mind answering your question. I'm going to have to kill both of you. You will get off the island, just as you wished, but you will not return, nor will you make the mainland. Does that answer your question?" His smile was oily, eyes hard and cruel. "It will seem an accident. The two of you went boating and well, accidents do happen, don't they? Nothing messy like last night, or like what happened to Judy. Both of those were careless. We can't afford many more mistakes like those. Oh, yes, you will have two friends with you, Curly and Shirley—they were

144

with you...boating. Your bodies will never be found. Just missing...I'll make a report later in the day to the Coast Guard and maybe they'll come out and give us a hand in finding you—but of course we'll find nothing."

He opened the door with a grand motion as the foreign man pocketed his gun. "Just don't make the mistake of attempting to escape. We'll be going out the back way and if we happen to bump into any-body, be smart and play it cool, my children."

Leaving the house was depressingly easy; no-body crossed our path. Once outside, I found it im-possible to keep from asking: "You wouldn't recon-sider your plans?"

"Surely Mr. Williamson, you don't take me for a fool."

"You know that, too?"

"We heard all. I was wondering about you from the beginning, though. That's why I was most anx-ious for you to see Gale—for she has a way of get-ting information from a man, without even asking a question—as you have discovered."

"What really happened to Judy? That's the least you can give me."

"Why?"

"You have my payment for two months lodging in cash...if for no other reason."

"That's true. But have you ever had more fun for so little in your life?"

MURDER MOST TERRIBLE! BY CHARLES NUETZEL

Chapter Sixteen

"I think it's costing a lot."

"Like they say, some men live a fast life and...well, you can't have them all." His laughter was cutting.

We were now making our way along the path that led to the cove below. The sun was bright in the sky and it was hard to believe that I would never see it setting. One has a very difficult time imagining and accepting his own end; even under such obvious circumstances. Something had to be done to reverse our situation. My mind flitted through countless means of gaining the advantage; the training and experience that South Viet Nam duty had given me were all I had to fall back on.

"You wouldn't mind telling me what we're dying for?" I continued the perversely casual conversation.

"Of course not. But obviously you won't be able to get all the details—a mere outline, since your time is running out." Andy King's voice was quite friendly, much as if he were carrying on a conversation with a friend who was about to take a pleasure trip. "In the first place, your sister saw things that were none of her business and she threatened to report to the others and then to the authorities—just who *those* might be she seemed to be quite vague about, under the circumstances."

"There are such organizations as the CIA," I suggested.

"There are. Your friend Curly was a member of such. Thus it was necessary to...arrange his disappearance, which, I'm sorry to say, you happened to witness. But...some people just have all the bad luck in one day." He chuckled as if at a private joke.

"You still haven't said *what* it is that you're involved in."

"One might call it foreign trade—much like most private governments. And you might call Eros a private little government. After all, we are in International waters and we do not recognize any national government. When I set this thing up I was very careful about that. You might call us something like the little mouse that roared."

"Rat, sounds more like it," I couldn't help commenting.

"Have it your own way. It is all the same. Everybody has a right to look at things their own way. It so happens that I believe that adult people should have the right and real freedom to live the kind of life they most desire. If it is free love or free narcotics or free LSD or what. Coke; real coke! Big bucks in that. Far more than you jerks pay to be part of this Eros cult—which is a great, grand cover and...well, it does kinda work in a nice way...for all concerned."

"So that's it?" I inquired as we started down the stone pathway to the beach below.

"A part of it; a very small part of it. Let's just

148

say I'm a very practical business man. I believe that so-called sin is going to go on no matter what kinds of laws are made against it. People will be people and, until you change them, you can't do a thing about vice or perversion or hatred just by passing a law. There are people who hate sex, or liquor, or Japanese, narcotics, smoking, races. Black, green, brown, yellow, red. And no law or social order will change things easily. We have hate bread into us from childhood. Bias. You name it. Difficult to change what is in the hearts of men. And religion of all kinds can bread blind faith in false systems—no matter what you call it! Hate is sold by governments and churches. They all claim they're the good ones and all others are the demons to be hated. Kill all the outsiders and protect the clan. Only time will change that. And there are those who have run out of time—who do not want to wait. So, because of that we have problems. But no matter. The point is there are people who want things and they will always find a way to get them. I'm willing to be one of the suppliers, since there is a lot of money to be made in such an occupation and my not doing it will not stop the process. If you can't stop them, join them, I've always believed. The human race if filled with nothing but suckers. They were born to be sucked dry, used and abused. They are blind fools. And people like me make use of their blind foolishness."

I found it impossible to avoid one blast back at King. "Like all the double-talk you give the Eros crowd, twisting in even a sense of religion, there's just enough logic to your acid thinking to make it *sound* logical. You have a way with words, King.

But you don't really think straight."

"My friend, history is filled with winners and losers—the winners are *always* right, the losers are always wrong. The winners are always good, and great and perfect, white gods, and the losers are always bad, mean and black devils. If Hitler had won WWII, what he did to the Jews would have been written down in history books as a footnote, as was what happened to the Christians during the Roman times. All that would truly be remembered would be the works of art that would have come from the German culture over the years—as with Rome. People come and go—countless millions, every generation—and it doesn't really matter to the universe what they did in their lifetimes to each other. The universe doesn't really care. We're living on a very small planet. What happens here, even after Man is gone, will be recorded for a short time on the face of the planet we call Earth and then fade away. The universe will continue on and on and it won't matter. I'm merely realistic."

"For Andy King. First, last and always, right?" I commented bitterly, as we stepped out onto the sand.

"For myself, yes. As all of us are. If you had a chance you would kill me right now to save your own little unimportant skin. If you die, nobody will really suffer too much. If I die, those people whom I supply with joy, not only on Eros but all over the North American Continent, would suffer."

"Not really, King. There would be somebody else to take your place."

"A good point. But it would take time."

"Not as long as you think. This friend of yours

here, who speaks so silently with a gun and knife, would probably he quite happy to take over your work."

King glanced at his foreign friend. "Karl Schults, a Neo-Nazi—what we used to call a bad German—there are really only a few so-called bad Germans, you know. Most of them are just people like us, human beings who can be led. And they were led down a path of terror and horror. I'll admit that. The truth is that people are pure asses—you can't trust any of them. A Hitler here cause world war, a Nero there to burn Rome, a Stalin to…well you get the idea. Even mother-in-laws…or their counter-part father-in-laws. You name it! A brutal husband or cold wife. A rapist. Serial killer. The monsters exist everywhere in our society for a flashing moment and leave their mark. For a moment they exist on this planet and then they are gone. Puff! Gone and forgotten. As you will soon be. Nobody will miss you—well, not for long. And it won't matter, anyway. So there are good people and bad people and good Americans and bad Americans. But which are the bad ones? Which are the good ones? Only history records that, and winners write history books! People are led by leaders…down a rosy path."

"Led to send people to the gas ovens, or chop, chop their heads off…you mean?" I countered, pointedly.

"No…just people who needed to survive. Those people who fight for your side may be called Freedom Fighters, but to their enemies they are called terrorist. Those revolutionist who helped to create our nation, out of the British Colonies here in America, were considered terrorist by the English authorities. It has nothing to do with right or wrong so much as it has to do with winners and losers. Historically, as a prime example of a popular monster, in Germany during the early part of the twentieth century, Hitler took over when the world in general was having an upheaval, and Germany was feeling the defeat of WWI pretty hard. Hitler promised work for the masses, and gave them work, the results of which are still in existence in a now unified Germany."

"Yes, like what was left of the bombed-out cities?"

"No, like lakes, roads, things like that. From every bad government comes good, too. The people followed the person who could feed their children's mouths—at first they didn't care who it was when they learned the truth, it was too late. No, there are very few men like this fellow here—there are very few Nazis in the world like him. They died with Hitler—either in spirit or in body. I don't worry about him."

We had now reached the sandy beach and moved across it to a small section where a boat was awaiting us at the end of a dock.

Well," King announced, "your time is limited and I must say that I'm sorry that things turned out so bad for you—but circumstances make it necessary to see to it that you can not use the information you have discovered about us. Some things are more important than a few people's lives. Sorry for you, my friend." Then King glanced at Sue Kong. "As for you, it is a pity, for you are a very lovely girl and I hate seeing lovely girls killed, too many have already suffered because they had noses that started scenting news that was none of their business. So, it cannot be helped."

We reached the small motorboat, at the bottom of which were the bodies of Curly and the young woman I had seen King walk off with. Both were dead.

King said something to Schults in German, which I couldn't understand, and then the man jerked the gun up high above my head, slammed it down hard.

Black spurted around my brain like the quick explosion of some giant star that leaves nothing but darkness in its place.

My first awareness after being knocked unconscious by Schults was the sensation of rocking. At first I couldn't remember what had happened last. The rocking continued back and forth, seeming to keep time with the pain throbbing at the back of my head. Finally I managed to open my eyes and found myself looking up into the sun. Turning, moaning, I looked about me and remembered what had happened last. The amazing thing was that I still lived.

When I attempted to move, I realized that my hands were tied behind me.

Sue Kong's voice sounded from my left: "I wasn't sure if they had killed you or not. That bad man hit you pretty hard."

I rolled over and found Sue Kong lying on her side, looking at me. She was bound hand and foot.

"What happened?"

MURDER MOST TERRIBLE! BY CHARLES NUETZEL

Chapter Seventeen

"They hit you, then tied the two of us and set a charge to blow the boat up in twenty minutes after it left shore." Her voice was emotionless, her face drawn tight with fear, the flesh almost white.

"How much time do we have?"

"Not much. You remained unconscious for a long while."

"Well, I don't plan on just dying without a try...slip over here close. Sue, do you have strong teeth?"

She moved closer, as instructed, but looked puzzled at my question.

"I want you to attempt to loosen my bonds—the knots—with your teeth. It's probably the only chance we have, do you understand?"

She nodded and immediately began to slip downwards, an awkward struggle, until her mouth was at my wrists.

"If we can get me loose," I told her in a calm voice, "there's a chance we might be able to get out of this thing...at least we have to try."

Sue didn't say a word but started to work on the ropes about my wrists.

I encouraged her by saying, "They probably

didn't expect me to regain consciousness before the boat blew up—so we have a good chance!" I was trying to sound as certain as possible. I didn't have much hope, but in any case, there was always a slim chance—and if we were to die, at least her attempts to free me would keep her mind occupied until the explosion took place.

I continued to talk as she worked, to give her mind something else to consider. "Once we get out of this, we'll have to report to the authorities...I don't know what they can do about it, but they have to do something—somehow.

"If that doesn't work, then we have to go back and take care of King ourselves. If the law won't touch King in international waters, then they won't touch me if I kill him. Probably the government would be quite happy if I did kill him."

I could feel that the ropes about my wrists were slowly beginning to loosen. Hope began to surge through me. But we didn't know how much time we had. That time limit was the most terrible thing about the situation.

"The minute you have me free, I'm going to get the explosives off. Immediately—not now—after I'm free, you shout where the explosives are. I'll move, fast. Everything will depend on our moving with the quickest amount of speed. It's the only chance we have. So, don't hesitate. The minute your work is finished, tell me where the explosives are."

Suddenly the rope seemed to slip slightly and I heard a sigh of frustration come from Sue.

"I can't do it," she announced.

"Come on, keep trying. I think in just a moment..."

Her teeth once more grabbed hold of the knotted rope.

After what seemed like hours, and couldn't have been more than a few minutes, the rope loosened a little more. This time I struggled as Sue stopped to get her breath.

Almost immediately the rope seemed to loosen, but not enough.

"Sue." It was all I needed to say. Sue was once again at the ropes.

Sweat was dripping down my forehead, my thoughts felt as if they were being pressured by some invisible claw attempting to bring panic to them. Time. We just didn't have much. Would it be enough?

Then suddenly a sigh of relief sounded from Sue, and I strained on the rope that easily came loose. Hands free, I untied my feet, said: "Where?"

"Under the controls!"

I tore the ropes from about my ankles and then staggered to my feet. Everything seemed prickly, as if my muscles had gone to sleep, but I ignored this as every effort centered on reaching the controls.

At first I didn't see anything out of line.

"The panel, under the controls!" Sue screamed.

Then I saw a metal plate and fairly clawed at it. The panel quickly slid to one side and then I saw the small little time bomb; crude, but effective. Grabbing it, I turned, hefted the bomb in my right hand and flung it out over the side of the ship. It was high in the air, some twenty yards away when suddenly an explosion rocked the ocean air like white blue fire that gushed blood. The boat rocked and I was flung off my feet.

A moment later I worked on Sue Kong's ropes, freeing her. She immediately came into my arms, trembling, sobbing, her head against my chest.

There is a time and place for love and a time and place for action. We found ourselves pressed by the necessity of taking immediate action against King, yet the nearness of that lovely, delicate form was startlingly exciting. The aftermath of facing death, of almost having it choke our throats in its clutching hands, seemed to develop a keen need to prove we were still alive. It is the only explanation that I can give for what we did.

Sue looked up at me, her lips trembling, eyes haunted, arms about my waist. We were half lying, half sitting on the floor of the small boat. I could feel the pressure of her breasts against me and the warmth of her body. Suddenly her lips moved upwards and they were under mine, warm and moist, the tears still streaming down her cheeks as her tongue surged deep into my mouth. Her body strained to mine and there was no guessing about what was going to happen.

My right hand found her breast, fondled, caressed. A moan passed from her lips as the kiss broke and she pulled me down onto the floor of the boat, locking her body to mine

The very insanity of our situation brought on a madness that blurred most of the first moments. I know that somehow I managed to get her clothing off. She helped as I pulled the bra from her breasts, she lifted up as my fingers slipped under the little lacy panties about her hips. She trembled as my hand raced gently across her legs, then dipped down to explore the soft warmth between her thighs. She moaned, grabbed at my shoulders, drew me down to her breasts, and for the first time I realized that I was naked, too, but couldn't remember having undressed. As I cupped one breast in my hands, lowered my lips to enclose the hardened nipple in a voluptuous kiss, I felt her hands reach down along my body, searching for the tight pain that knotted into a spear-like weapon below my waist. Then her fingers found what she was searching for and her hips trembled, surged upwards as I felt the urgent call of her pull me into the hot warmth of her. Legs wrapped about my legs, arms embraced me, now, as I kissed her face, her lips, and eyes throat. That first beautiful moment as we were totally united, that first wonderful joy of feeling this woman holding me in her, savoring the pleasure that our union afforded, was overwhelming, yet we did not move for some time; but just lay there, locked together. Finally it was impossible to control the urgent need, the crying lust that demanded movement.

We had both been waiting for this moment, this joining of our flesh in such joyous intimacy, since we had first met. And it had built throughout those hours to this very instant.

I lifted slowly and experienced such joy that it was impossible to wait longer. Yet I kept up a slow, torturous movement, savoring every moment as if it were some wonderful eternity from which we would never escape. I didn't want it to end; I didn't want to ever leave Sue Kong's body. I wanted this to last forever; for this was the only total conviction that I still lived, still breathed, was not dead in some heavenly grave.

Sue moaned with every move I made. In the end

she was clawing at me with frantic desperation, her hips driving upwards in perfect rhythm with my own. Finally we strained together and then after what seemed a very long time, the two of us slowly parted, lying side-by-side on the bottom of the boat that was supposed to have been our funeral coffin.

It wasn't until some time later that I realized that two dead bodies had been witness to our carnal act.

We were gathering up our clothing, silently starting to get dressed, when the sound of a boat coming our way brought my attention to the horizon. If it hadn't been coming from the opposite direction from Eros, I might have believed that King was on his way to prove he'd accomplished his mission: our death.

The two of us had just finished getting dressed when I realized that the boat was a Coast Guard cruiser, heading in our direction, obviously investigating the explosion.

Upon realization of this, I became painfully conscious of the fact that there were two dead bodies on board our boat. How were we to explain them?

This realization caused me to feel no great joy about the immediate meeting with the U. S. Coast Guard. If we had called to them for help, it might have been different. Instead they were about to discover us, and what would they say about our story? Could they believe us? I suddenly realized that it was quite a story I had to tell, one that would be difficult to swallow; especially with the evidence of two bodies on board to make it seem even more fantastic.

I waited, arm about Sue Kong, feeling total defeat, as the Coast Guard cruiser approached.

MURDER MOST TERRIBLE! BY CHARLES NUETZEL

Chapter Eighteen

Life is so full of letdowns that one sometimes forgets that the unexpected can also be pleasant.

Sue Kong was leaning against me, her hips touching mine, the sweet scent of her in my nostrils, her wonderful body close to mine. Eros seemed so close, yet light-years away. We stood there waiting for the Coast Guard to approach, knowing what they would find and wondering whether they would believe our story. But everything turned out better than expected.

The last place I thought the two of us would be that evening, was in a motel room together. The last place I expected to be spending the afternoon was in a small L.A. office, near Main and 19th Street, two grim-faced men firing questions at me until my voice was a rasping grate, my vocal cords painful knots that found words hard to form.

The order of events were as follows:

The Coast Guard approached, boarded, discovered the two bodies, took us into custody; the commanding officer demanded an explanation, which we gave in full, merely keeping the sexual material edited out of our story. Checking up on Curly was easy enough, a call to their top ranking commanders, a call to CIA, and then a return call to the cruiser as it was making its way back to the coast. Course was changed and the police were waiting for us as we docked in the Marina Del Rey. Sue was taken in one car and they shoved me in the back seat of another police car. At the Santa Monica Police Station I was turned over to two men dark suits that looked as if they had been slept in for weeks. They drove me in total silence to Los Angeles, came to a stop in front of a small, depressing looking building, escorted me to a small room and started firing questions that forced total recall of the events on Eros. I kept asking about Sue, but was told to answer the questions, not ask them. When I demanded a lawyer, they shook their heads, said there was nothing to worry about. When I asked for cigarettes, one of them left, returning later with a carton.

"Tell it to us again," they demanded, and I repeated myself. When my experiences on Eros Island had been related half a dozen times, they sat back in their wooden chairs and the tallest one said: "Will you repeat all this in court?"

I nodded, lit a cigarette and eyed the tall man, who was called Jack. "With pleasure. But what can you do to King? He's out in international waters."

"Legally it is a tricky thing. But there are ways and if it weren't for these rather unconventional methods...well, the world would not be quite as safe to live in. Criminals use the law to protect themselves—sometimes the law has to use its own methods to stop those criminals. The man you knew as Curly Davis was one of us...and we've been trying to line up a case against King for some years. Your testimony—coupled with that of Miss Kong—will place him right in our hands."

Like a fool, I asked: "You wouldn't be needing any help, would you?"

They gave me a mystified look.

"Well, King is a dirty old man who did a few things against my family—like killing my sister and trying to kill me—I would like very much to put my fingers around his neck and squeeze him to death."

They laughed. "Not like the books," the older one announced. "You've done all you're going to do. The rest is up to men like us. King is involved with international smuggling, dope, you name it...government secrets—anything he can sell. We need him whole and alive...to pick his brain, you might say."

"You don't mind if I pick his body a bit, before-hand, do you?"

"No dice. Men are already on their way to the island to make arrangements to bring King back to the States, where he can be tried for murder, among other things."

I felt a sense of disappointment, but at the same time a feeling of release and relief.

"You mean," I retorted with some humor in my voice, "that I don't get to go into hand-to-hand combat with King—like they do on television?"

"In court. There will be the battle— and you can bet your life it will be a hard one. You've done just about all you can. Just don't go running out of town—okay?"

I shrugged, grinned, started to stand, hesitated, and then stood when they didn't make any attempt to restrain me. My body was cramped from sitting on the chair for such a long time.

"I must admit," I told the two men, "I'm a little let-down. All the stories I read, the hero has to fight his way out, tooth and nail, is almost defeated and then hammers the villain to unconsciousness in the last pages."

"In stories. In life it doesn't always work out that way. And, in any case, I should think you've had enough action for one day." The men both grinned.

I wanted to see Sue Kong.

"Where's the girl?" I asked.

"In the room down the hall. You can go out and wait for her, if you like," Jack told me, grinning toothily. "That's one reward you get that guys in our business aren't so lucky to enjoy. We have to keep working on the case...you can go out and forget the whole thing, enjoy yourself—no bruises, no gun wounds, no danger. You're the lucky one."

Sue was waiting for me in the hall, and the two of us left the building, hand in hand.

We both needed a drink and found the nearest bar. After that a phone call got us a cab and the cab took us to the hotel. The rest was up to us.

During the next six months, Sue Kong was my sole companion. They were nice, easy, swinging months; except for the court room scenes. In the end, King was given his due reward, the CIA was given its due reward in information, Eros was closed forever, and now lies on the blue Pacific in a quite death; a tomb, empty and lifeless. Sue, like most women who pass through a man's life, disappeared into the background, naturally. We parted true friends, going our separate ways as lovers many times do when they have run the course of their affair. It was a wonderful time, and we truly enjoyed every moment together.

As for myself, you might meet me under different names, hear different stories about my so-called past life—but none of it would be true. I made some smart connections and joined a very secret division of the government; much like that which had, in the end, crushed King's Eros Cult. Since then I managed to fade into the international scene. Call me a spy or secret agent of whatever your imagination might supply; but you'll never really guess the truth. The fact is, that my life has flowered into quite a series of adventures far more rewarding than my experiences on Eros. Eros was the beginning of a long series of actions against the evil doers of the world and in learning about Man and his perverse ways.

Enough to simply note it has been a wonderfully rewarding couple of decades since the events on Eros. And life has been wonderful.

About the Author

Charles Nuetzel was born in San Francisco in 1934, and writes:

"As long as I can remember I wanted to be a writer. It was a dream I never thought would materialize. But with the help of Forrest J Ackerman, who became my agent, I managed to finally make it into print.

"I was lucky enough not only in selling my work to publishers but also ending up packaging books for some of them, and finally becoming a 'publisher' much like those who had bought my first novels. From there it as a simple leap to editing not only a sci-fi anthology, but a line of sci-fi books for Powell Sci-Fi back in the 1960s. Throughout these active professional years I had the chance to design some covers and do graphic cover layouts for pocket books & magazines."

Much of his work in covers and graphics are a result of having had a father who was a professional commercial artist, and who did a number of covers for sci-fi magazines in the 1950s and later for pocket books—even for some of Mr. Nuetzel's books.

In retirement he has become involved in swing dancing, a long time lover of Big Band jazz. But more interestingly world travels have taken him (and his wife Brigitte) across the world, to Hawaii, Caribbean, Mexico, Kenya, Egypt, Peru, having a lifelong interest in ancient civilizations. His website is full of thousands of pictures taken during these trips.

www.ingramcontent.com/pod-product-compliance
Lightning Source LLC
Chambersburg PA
CBHW020617250626
47154CB00004B/1553